CYBER

SURFERS

4

CYBERCOPS & FLAME WARS

Written by Ted Pedersen
& Mel Gilden

PRICE STERN SLOAN®
Los Angeles

Where to go online for more cool Internet information!

The Putnam Berkley Group offers a list of books available at: http://www.putnam.com

And MCA/Universal Cyberwalk World Wide Web site has fun entertainment information at: http://www.mca.com

Cover Designed by Sheena Needham
Cybersurfers Series Concept Copyright © 1996 Price Stern Sloan, Inc.
Text copyright © 1996 Mel Gilden and Ted Pedersen
Cover illustration copyright © 1995 Geoffrey Gove
Published by Price Stern Sloan, Inc.,
A member of The Putnam & Grosset Group,
New York, New York.

Library of Congress Cataloging-in-Publication Data

Pedersen, Ted.
    Ghost on the Net / by Ted Pedersen and Mel Gilden.
    p. cm.—(Cybersurfers; #4)
    Summary: Athena becomes entangled in an Internet "flame war," and enlists her friend Jason to help stop the escalating problems that result.
    ISBN 0-8431-3979-X
    [1. Internet (Computer network)—Fiction.
2. Computers—Fiction.
3. Ghosts—Fiction. 4. Family life—Fiction.]
I. Gilden, Mel. II. Title. III. Series.
PZ7.P3424Cy 1996
[Fic]—dc20
                         94-34655
                              CIP
                              AC

First Edition   ISBN 0-8431-3979-X

10 9 8 7 6 5 4 3 2 1

Welcome to Cyberspace!
You are now online.
Please type in your password.

Jason Kane and Athena Bergstrom know the ins and outs of surfing the Net better than anyone at their school. They also know the netiquette of surfing, the rules about what is cool in cyberspace—and what is not.

When Athena gets a flame from an obnoxious person online who refers to himself as Rebel, she responds exactly as she shouldn't: She flames him right back.

Soon her family starts getting nasty phone calls and her father's credit is destroyed. Using the Net to hack his way through Athena's life, Rebel is totally out of control. And when a new girl at school with great computer skills seems to be succeeding in capturing Jason's attention, Athena's world gets grim.

Will she and Jason be able to hack their way out of the mess Rebel has created? Read on, cybersurfers!

Attention User:
This is the first series to combine new technologies with exciting adventure! Complete glossary of Internet signs and computer terms included for all newbies.

DEDICATION

To David Bishoff—writer, hacker, and friend.
—Ted
For Susie Miller—my favorite hacker.
—Mel

Cybersurfers

1

chapter one@cybersurfers.cybercops
chapter one@cybersurfers.cybercops
chapter one@cybersurfers.cybercops

Jason Kane was so involved in setting up his computer that when he turned around, he was surprised to see the crowd that now filled the big multi-purpose room. He normally avoided crowds, but he had to make an exception for the Fort Benson High School Open House.

"Quite a zoo," he commented to the young woman working nearby. Athena Bergstrom, one of his few real friends, had short dark hair, and almost never failed to wear jeans and a flannel lumberjack shirt. Their first impressions of one another had been indifference, but the two of them had been thrown together in so many Internet adventures that they'd actually bonded. If anyone was more amazed by this than Jason, it was probably Athena herself.

Now Athena took a step back to study what was on the monitor of the computer she'd been

Don't know what a word means?
Check Internet notes on page 129.

laboring over. "What do you think?" she asked Jason as she stared critically at the screen, her head cocked to one side.

On the screen a photograph of a famous actor was slowly morphing into the face of a lion. The lion transformed into a picture of Mr. Madison, their computer lab teacher. Mr. Madison then became an elephant. Jason was fascinated by the constantly changing video. Athena was better at creating computer art than anyone else he knew.

"Da bomb," Jason said appreciatively.

"Not groovy?" Athena asked, smiling.

"Nothing has been *groovy*," Jason assured her, "since 1972. Get a load of this."

Athena came over and looked at his screen. A haunted house sat on a creepy, moonlit hill. A boy and girl were walking up the steps toward the haunted house.

"This is the Cyberhut. The online kids' forum I'm creating for the school."

"Cute," Athena said. "What does it do?"

"Try it and find out."

Athena took the mouse and used it to move the girl up the stairs and then, as the door creaked open, into the house. Now the screen image changed to the house's interior, and the girl was greeted by a butler who looked like a movie monster version of a servant.

"Pretty impressive," Athena said.

They both jumped as a group of people who had gathered behind them applauded. Athena joined in the applause and Jason beamed.

After a few minutes, when it was clear nothing else would happen on the computer screen, the crowd drifted away.

"It looked pretty good," Jason admitted, "but the transformation from outside to inside took too long. It should have been smoother."

"Do you think anybody else will notice?"

"That doesn't matter," Jason insisted. "I noticed."

"Same way with my art," Athena agreed. "I have to be satisfied with it before I show it to anybody else." Athena went back to her own exhibit. Jason was left facing a tall, slim young woman with long blond hair. She wore jeans and a Pearl Jam T-shirt.

"Hey, Susan," Jason said. "You getting around all right?" Susan had just transferred from out of town. She was a babe and had an interest in computers, too. Just watching her stand there was kind of exciting to Jason.

"Better than I expected," Susan said. "What are you doing?"

"Just fixing a glitch."

"I might be able to take care of that for you," she suggested and took a step closer.

"No thanks," Jason replied as he sat down again at his computer and began to type code. "It's my own programming cute. I—uh—I mean code," he stammered. "No one else knows it." He didn't know why she made him so nervous, but he was suddenly sweating bullets.

"Problem?" a young man asked Jason.

Jason looked up and saw a tall dude standing next to Susan. Jason felt his jaw suddenly clench. He stood and hooked his thumbs into the front pockets of his jeans. "What do you want, Bruce?"

asked Jason, frowning tensely.

Bruce had bushy red hair and wore the same thing nearly every day. His uniform consisted of black jeans and various T-shirts with a yellow lightning bolt across the front. On his breast pocket was stitched an old-fashioned bit key and the words, LOCK-ME-TIGHT SYSTEMS.

Bruce wore a small, self-satisfied smile that Jason had come to hate. "Just here to see the open house," he said.

"Here it is," Jason said.

Bruce stepped forward and peered at the Cyberhut screen. "I saw the demonstration you did for Athena and noticed you had a glitch in your timing."

"Works for me," Jason said.

"Kids," Bruce said as he smiled at Susan and shrugged as if he were saying, Can you believe this guy? There's no teaching him.

Jason wanted to punch him. "Kid, huh?" Jason replied sarcastically. Who did this guy think he was anyway? Actually, he knew who Bruce thought he was. They'd met the week before in the office of the school principal, Ms. O'Malley...

Mr. Madison had called him and Athena out of computer lab. They wouldn't miss much. They already knew more than most of the other kids anyway.

"Where are we going?" Jason had asked as they walked down the empty hall. Behind the closed doors, classes were in session.

"Ms. O'Malley wants to see us," replied Mr. Madison.

"She's not going to tell us again how she got

along without computers, and how we can, too, is she?" Athena asked, rolling her eyes.

Jason chuckled. "Maybe she wants us to save data by rubbing two punch cards together." If Ms. O'Malley had her way, they'd all still be sending smoke signals and using slide rules.

"Oh, Ms. O'Malley is all right," Mr. Madison assured them. "No, she just has a visitor she wants us all to meet."

When they entered Ms. O'Malley's office, Bruce Archer was already there, sitting in an armchair, wearing the same outfit he would wear while visiting the open house—or one just like it. Though he wasn't much older than a high-school graduate, he had the air of an adult.

"This is my nephew, Bruce Archer," Ms. O'Malley had said proudly, and made introductions all around. Bruce shook hands with each of them. There was nothing wrong with shaking hands, of course; it just wasn't something Jason usually did with people near his own age.

"You're looking well today, sir," Bruce said to Mr. Madison. "My aunt has told me how bright you are," he said to Jason in a condescending way. Then Bruce turned to Athena and said, "Charmed, I'm sure." Athena smiled at Bruce. Jason didn't like the way he kept staring at her.

What a brown-noser, Jason thought to himself. Bruce seemed to be putting on some sort of an act.

"I've asked Bruce to help you with your open house projects," Ms. O'Malley said.

"Auntie twisted my arm," Bruce said and smiled at Ms. O'Malley.

Jason frowned. He wanted to tell Ms. O'Malley

what he thought of Bruce's help, but rather than blowing up in her face he decided it would be safer to let Mr. Madison handle the situation.

"We appreciate your concern," Mr. Madison said, "but we have the situation pretty well under control."

"I'm sure we could all learn a thing or two from you, sir," Bruce oozed.

"Bruce is studying computer science at Stanford. He has a summer job up here with Lock-Me-Tight Systems," Ms. O'Malley explained. "He knows quite a bit about computers."

"Lock-Me-Tight?" Athena asked.

"It's security, Athena," Bruce replied. "We design and implement corporate computer system security. It's a pretty specialized field."

Jason had always heard good things about Lock-Me-Tight Systems, but he wasn't about to admit that to Bruce. "I've heard of them," he said. "They build firewalls."

"Among other things," Bruce added.

"I think it's important for our students to set up their own exhibits," Mr. Madison said. "After all, the open house is supposed to give the outside world an idea what we're doing in our classes."

Besides, Jason thought, he didn't want some professional cybercop looking over his shoulder while he tinkered with his project.

Ms. O'Malley nodded, considering what Mr. Madison had said. Jason noticed Bruce looking at Athena again. Jason wondered if Bruce knew she wasn't just a piece of meat.

"Very well," Ms. O'Malley said at last.

"Please keep in mind that I'm available when

you need help," Bruce said.

"We really appreciate it," replied Athena with a small smile.

"That's the spirit," Bruce said, as he handed each of them one of his business cards. If Athena and Mr. Madison hadn't been present, Jason would have crumpled the card and tossed it into the waste basket. Instead he followed their lead and stuffed it into his pocket.

Athena, Jason, and Mr. Madison soon made their way into the hallway and walked slowly back to the computer lab. Mr. Madison chewed on his lower lip. He seemed thoughtful.

"Thanks for saving us from that guy," Jason said.

"I don't think he's so bad," Athena protested.

"What I said did the trick only because Ms. O'Malley knew I was right. There's no point having an open house unless you kids do your own work," Mr. Madison said, confirming Jason's opinion.

Jason nodded. He didn't care why Mr. Madison's argument did the trick as long as it kept Bruce Archer away from him. The guy gave him the definite creeps.

That had all happened a week ago, and since then none of them had had a reason to call Bruce. The truth was, Jason would have suffered torture by thumbscrews before he called Bruce for anything. Now Bruce had appeared at the open house—probably invited by Ms. O'Malley—and was tossing around little insults like cherry bombs.

"*I'm* calling you a kid, kid," Bruce said to

Jason. "But it's nothing personal." He indicated Jason's keyboard. "May I?" he asked, as he sat down and began to type.

"Hey," Jason cried, but it was already too late. Against his will, he was fascinated by what Bruce was doing.

"What's going on?" Susan asked.

"I'm tuning up the operating system," Bruce answered, looking up only long enough to smile graciously at Susan. "It should run faster now. Whaddya think?"

"It's OK," Jason said, though admitting even that much hurt him.

"Hey, Jason," Athena called out. She had found her parents and her older brother, Ralph. Mr. Bergstrom was a big man who looked a little uncomfortable in his sports coat. Ralph took after him, and Athena looked more like her mom, a small, thin woman. People who saw the family together for the first time wondered what Mr. and Mrs. Bergstrom saw in each other, but Jason knew that Mr. Bergstrom was not the gorilla he appeared to be, and Mrs. Bergstrom was pretty handy with a screwdriver. They had more in common than most people thought.

Bruce stood and lit up as if someone had plugged him in. "How nice to see you, Athena. These must be your parents?"

Jason stewed while Athena introduced her family to Bruce and Susan. Bruce shook hands with everybody.

"Come on, Jason," Athena said. "Want to help me show Ralph and my parents around the open house? Mr. Madison said he would watch our exhibits while we went."

"Great," Jason said, pleased to escape Bruce. He nodded at Susan and said, "Catch you later," as he walked away with Athena and her family.

"That Susan is a surfin' babe," Athena whispered to him.

"You think?" Jason said.

"What's the matter, Jason? A quart low on hormones today?"

"Hey look," Jason said suddenly. "Here's Tracy's diorama of the Battle of Bunker Hill."

"That's really something," Ralph commented, hunkering down to look across the large expanse of mud, papier-mâché, and toy soldiers. Tracy stood behind it, ready to explain everything. Like Susan, she was a blonde. But Tracy had no interest in computers, and as far as Jason could tell, no interest in him, either.

While he listened to Tracy talk about the Battle of Bunker Hill, Jason was aware that Athena was studying him closely. If she was worried he would run off with Susan, she could stop now. Jason didn't understand it himself, but he wasn't really interested in any girl but Athena. Sometimes the feeling bugged him, especially when they weren't getting along, but he couldn't change it.

"The Battle of Bunker Hill was actually fought on Breed's Hill in Massachusetts in 1775," Tracy explained. "Though the British won the battle, the Colonists were encouraged by their own bravery and continued the Revolution."

"Wow," Ralph exclaimed a little too effusively for Jason's taste. "You did all this yourself?"

"My dad helped a little."

"Wow," Ralph repeated.

Athena knew that Tracy frequently reduced men to single syllables, but she was surprised it happened to Ralph.

"Come on, Ralph," Mrs. Bergstrom said.

"You go ahead," Ralph said. "I'll catch up." The art department was displaying paintings and sculptures, the home economics department was selling cupcakes, and the English department had a display table with books that had been banned by various organizations over the decades. But the strangest exhibit by far was in the vacant field just outside the multi-purpose room. It was a helicopter. A fully equipped, U.S. Army helicopter. Four shy young guys dressed in green fatigues were standing in front of it, ready to answer any questions.

"What's all this," Mrs. Bergstrom asked.

"We're doing maneuvers in your area," one of the young soldiers said, "and we want you to know about it."

"Can I go inside the helicopter?" Jason asked immediately.

"Afraid not," the soldier said. "If you were to touch the wrong switch, you could really hurt somebody."

"Cool," Jason said. What must it be like to have the power of a group like the U.S. Army behind you? he wondered.

"What is your objective?" Mr. Bergstrom asked.

"Only our commanding officer knows," replied the soldier. "We'll find out what's going on when he starts giving orders."

"Sealed orders, eh?" Mr. Bergstrom asked.

"In a manner of speaking, sir. Actually, I understand the colonel is receiving his orders by computer."

Mr. Bergstrom shook his head. "What is the Army coming to?" he said. It was a well-known fact that Mr. Bergstrom didn't think much of computers. He let Athena have one only because she used it to keep the books for his gas station.

"Don't blow up the town," Mrs. Bergstrom said and laughed.

The soldiers politely laughed with her. "No, ma'am," one of them said. "The Army has a private staging area outside of town where we do our maneuvers."

Jason looked at his watch and was shocked to see that he and Athena had been away from their exhibits for almost an hour. "Come on, Ath," he said. "Mr. Madison has things to do besides watch our exhibits."

"Right." Athena hugged her mom and dad. "When Ralph comes up for air, say goodbye to him for me," she said as Jason led her away. It was getting late and the crowd was already thinning out. Still, the open house was supposed to go on for another forty-five minutes, and Jason felt obligated to do his part.

Not much was happening at the computer lab exhibit. Mr. Madison was sitting on a folding chair between the two computers. Jason was sorry to see that Susan wasn't there, but he was pleased to see that Bruce had gone.

"Are you alone?" Jason asked Mr. Madison.

"Just me and my memories," the computer teacher responded. "Why?"

"Bruce was here," Jason explained.

"I see. Well, the open house is almost over. You'll probably never see him again." Mr. Madison stood up. "You two can start packing up any time, I think the rush is over. I'm going to go see if home ec has any cupcakes left." He strolled off whistling.

Athena went to her computer, leaving Jason alone with his. Jason contemplated the Cyberhut home page. Bruce Archer was quite a hacker, there was no doubt about it. They might have actually gotten along if Bruce hadn't also been a first class jerk—sucking up to the adults and putting down his peers. Jason wondered what he had been like in high school. Probably worse, he decided.

"Jason," Athena called, "come and look at this!"

Jason went over to have a look. Athena was stiff with rage.

"What's up?" he asked.

She said nothing, but pointed to the e-mail message on her screen:

```
Dear Athena,
You're kind of cute,
but your art sucks transistors. :-,
            —Rebel
```

Jason shook his head. "Don't pay any attention to that flame." Jason said. "You know that flaming is done by jerks who have no life. Forget it."

"How did this jerk get my address?"

"It's not exactly a secret," Jason replied. "You can find anyone on the Internet—if you look hard enough in the right places. As long as they're not hiding behind a security firewall."

"OK," Athena said, trying to calm down. "But leaving a message like that is totally juvenile."

"Then forget it."

"I would . . . except for this." Athena touched a key on her board, and her morphing program came up again. Only this time the famous actor had a crudely scribbled patch over one eye, the lion had a crew cut, Mr. Madison had a crooked scar on one cheek, and the elephant had a really bad word scrawled on its trunk.

"This idiot defiled my artwork!" Athena said bitterly. "That's much worse than any stupid flame." They silently watched the morphing series cycle. Rebel had added something to each picture.

"You have a right to be upset," Jason said, "but what are you going to do? Flaming him back will just give him the satisfaction of knowing he rattled your cage."

"Hanging's too good for him," Athena grumbled.

"Let it be," Jason advised. "The less you give this guy to work with, the less chance he'll hit you again."

"Did you do this?" Athena accused, poking her finger into his chest with one hand and pointing to the screen with the other.

"Huh?"

Suddenly Athena's screen went blank and another message appeared:

Dear Cutie,
Catch me if you can! ;)
                    —Rebel

"You asked for it, brother," Athena said, and sat down at her keyboard.

"Whatever you have in mind, Ath," Jason warned, "you can't do it here. They're going to close up the whole building in less than an hour."

"Maybe I can borrow the Army's helicopter," Athena said.

"Maybe you better go home and chill out."

"What would you do if somebody did this to you?" Athena demanded.

Jason shrugged. "I guess I'd borrow the Army's helicopter and bomb the guy back to the Stone Age."

"So—"

"But that doesn't mean it's a good idea."

They watched the morphing program run. The damage to the video file looked permanent.

"You're right about them shutting down the building, anyway," Athena admitted. She punched off her computer and began to pack up her equipment.

Cybercops & Flame Wars

Jason went back to his own exhibit and began breaking it down. While he worked, he watched Athena angrily throw computer cables into a box. He knew she was not the kind of person who would take this sitting down. It was a challenge, and like him, Athena couldn't resist a challenge. Besides, along with her morphing video, her pride was hurt. He wondered who was going to end up in bigger trouble, Rebel—or Athena?

chapter two@cybersurfers.cybercops
chapter two@cybersurfers.cybercops
chapter two@cybersurfers.cybercops

Even after Athena had loaded all her computer equipment on the cart she was still angry. The physical labor of disconnecting everything, coiling the cables, loading the monitor, the CPU, and the keyboard onto the cart had allowed her to work off some of the heat of her anger. She now felt like a cool, dispassionate creature, but she still wanted revenge. The only remaining question was what form her revenge would take.

Athena pushed the loaded cart down the hall back to the computer lab when Tracy called to her. Athena really didn't want to talk to anybody, but Tracy was her best friend. And after all, Tracy wasn't Rebel. Probably not, anyway.

"You better hurry," Tracy said as she walked up. "Your family is waiting for you in front of the school, and your dad is making big noises about pizza."

"You coming, too?" Athena asked, teasing.

"Me?" Tracy asked with surprise. "Oh, you mean because of Ralph?" She laughed. "He's nice enough, but a little old. Besides, it would be just too weird to date your big brother."

"I guess," Athena said and walked on, a little annoyed that Tracy walked with her, still chattering about Ralph.

"Oh," Tracy said suddenly, "and if you want to reach me for the next week or so, call me at the Henderson's farm."

"What's happening there?"

"The Hendersons are going on vacation, and they hired me to house-sit."

"What about the cows and the pigs and the chickens?" Athena joked weakly.

"They don't have any, silly. It's a farm, but the Hendersons don't raise anything. They're retired."

I'm going to retire Rebel, but good, Athena thought. Just wait till I get home to my own computer. Athena went into the computer lab and put her equipment back onto her desk while Tracy waited for her outside. Jason's computer was already back in place, but he was nowhere to be seen. It would be like him not to hang around after an event was over.

"I guess I'll see you tomorrow," Athena told Tracy as she closed the computer lab door. Athena was the last one to return equipment so Mr. Madison could now lock up.

"Right," Tracy said, starting to walk away.

"I'll tell Ralph you said hello," Athena yelled over her shoulder as she hurried to the front of the school.

"Don't you dare!" Tracy called after her.

"Here she is, Little Miss Slowpoke," Ralph

called as Athena trotted down the front steps. The Pacific Northwest air was cold and transparent.

"I was putting away my computer," Athena explained as she joined her family. The school was deserted except for them.

"Who wants pizza?" Mr. Bergstrom asked.

"No thanks," Athena said.

"Are you sick?" Mrs. Bergstrom asked as she felt Athena's forehead.

"No," Athena said. "I just have some things to do at home." She squirmed a little, thinking about what she had in mind. It was amazing that she could be eager and uncomfortable at the same time. Rebel had to be stopped, that was for sure. But Athena was also sure there was a difference between justice and revenge. She generally knew it when she saw it, but not this time. The uncertainty was what made her squirm.

"What sort of things?" Ralph asked.

"Computer things," Athena said.

"Let's discuss it in the car," Mrs. Bergstrom said. "I'm freezing." They walked in a clump to the big old Chevy.

"Last chance. Anybody hungry?" Mr. Bergstrom asked from behind the wheel.

He, his wife, and his son raised their hands. Athena saw that she was doomed to eat pizza that evening whether she wanted it or not. Maybe she was a little hungry. "OK. But no anchovies," she said grumpily.

"No problem," Ralph said.

They went to Freddie's, of course. It was the only place in town that was still open and served a decent pizza. It was a friendly, old-fashioned, red-checkered–tablecloth kind of place, and Athena found it difficult to maintain her grump when embraced by the warm garlicky air.

Still, she didn't say much during the meal. She didn't even join in when her parents kidded Ralph about his interest in Tracy. She ate a lot of pizza though, and she found that the food fortified her spirit as well as her body. She became comfortable rather than desperate thinking about taking vengeance against Rebel.

"Are you all right?" her mother asked a couple of times.

"I'm fine," Athena insisted. "I just have this project on my mind."

"You're not in trouble are you?"

"Not at the moment," Athena said, trying to sound lighthearted.

Pizza at Freddie's seemed to take forever, but at last they were all finished and went out to the car—their breaths luminescent clouds in front of them—and drove home.

As the car pulled into the driveway and slowed to a stop, Athena couldn't stand waiting any longer. While Ralph and her parents were still getting out of the car, she bolted across the lawn to the front door. Of course, because she was in such a hurry, her key refused to fit into the lock.

"Try it this way," Ralph said, and opened the door on the first try. He looked smug, but then he didn't have Rebel on his mind.

Athena ran upstairs and threw her coat onto her bed as she crossed her bedroom. It's payback time, she thought as she booted up her computer. He who flames me is playing with fire.

Athena chuckled at her own wit. She was going to enjoy this.

The seconds before the computer screen flashed the familiar Windows™ logo seemed like hours. Patience, she told herself. Patience. You're acting like Jason. Of course, Jason had been the calm one so far. He'd been the one who told her that if she flamed him back, Rebel would have the satisfaction of knowing he'd yanked her chain. Jason was probably right, but he hadn't had a better idea. Besides, he'd admitted that if he had been Rebel's target he would have bombed Rebel back to the Stone Age. Say hello to one mad Homo sapien, Rebel, Athena thought to herself as she watched her computer do its thing.

She didn't really believe that Jason was Rebel. They had been through too much together, had become too close. Still, Jason had his maniacal side. They'd first met because he was dropping computer worms on her computer-generated rose garden. Was scribbling on her art really so different? Maybe he would laugh and show her how to instantly erase the graffiti. It didn't really matter. Whoever Rebel was, he was about to get a dose of his own medicine.

The computer finally beeped. It was ready. Athena used her mouse to double-click onto Icarus, her Internet gateway—the software that spoke to the computer that would hook her up to the Internet. Swiftly her gateway to the Net opened up and she was online.

***** CONNECT *****

Welcome to cyberspace. Enjoy your stay.
Is this business or pleasure?
Neither. It's revenge. Sweet revenge.

First find Rebel's home on the Net. Send a simple response to his original flame and see where it goes. Every piece of e-mail comes with a return address, though nothing guarantees that the return address is any more real than the handle the sender uses as a name.

It may have flickered, but the message goes nowhere. Or it went out and came back to where it started. Impossible to tell with this equipment and this software. But it's certain that the return address is a fake.

Not surprising. Rebel doesn't want people to know where he really lives.

But he's not perfect. He left tracks.

Jason taught her to look for them. Everyone leaves tracks. The trick is in finding them. Mailservers, the Internet's automated postal carriers, keep records. Check those. The real address will be in there somewhere.

Probably not even hidden. Probably stored in plain sight in such an obvious place it will be easily overlooked. Like the purloined letter in Edgar Allen Poe's story. Jason taught her that too.

Data scrolls on the screen. Begins to blur.

Go back. Look again. . . .
There! That's it. Click and capture.
You have Rebel's e-mail address!
It's a fake—but close enough to the real address
that you can mess up his Net-life.
Key in a nasty note:

  Rebel,
  Gotcha! You're not as hot as you thought.
  —Athena.   :-b

Send it once.
Now send it again.
Now send it a hundred times.
Should we try for a thousand?
No. No need to shout. Rebel made his point. You
made yours. All even.
This war is over.

***** DISCONNECT *****

Athena leaned back in her chair and smiled.
She felt the satisfaction that came with a job well
done. Rebel would think twice before rattling
her cage again. Jason had been worried over
nothing.

Athena was still proud of what she had done the
night before—not only tracked Rebel to his lair,

but given him a small taste of his own medicine. It had been a subtle operation, and she had handled it brilliantly. She told Tracy all about it on the way to school.

"So that's what you were upset about after the open house," Tracy exclaimed. "Why didn't you just tell me?"

"I guess I was embarrassed at being such a feeb."

"You're not a feeb anymore," Tracy said. "You sure stuck it to that Rebel guy."

Athena shook her head before she spoke again. "Jason wanted me to let the whole Rebel thing slide."

"Our Jason?"

"Amazing, huh? I guess he thought I might get hurt if Rebel turned out to be an eye-for-an-eye type. But I've been hanging around with him long enough to know what he would do if Rebel flamed him. Talking doesn't help with someone who won't listen—someone like Rebel."

"Jason was your inspiration. How romantic."

"Nothing romantic about it," Athena said, irritated that Tracy refused to understand about her and Jason. "We're a team. We're partners, at least when it comes to computers."

"How about when it comes to other things? Ever considered dating him?"

The idea had crossed Athena's mind. A couple of times she thought he had been on the verge of asking her out. Once she'd almost asked him. But she was afraid that getting involved romantically might break the spell, might spoil anything good they had together. And if they broke up, they might never be friends again. That was the last thing Athena wanted to happen.

Tracy nudged Athena out of her reverie with a sharp elbow. "Wake up, girl. You're staring at your competition."

Across the schoolyard, walking up the steps into the building was Susan Hunter.

"Do you think she's a babe?" Athena asked.

"More to the point," Tracy said, "does Jason think she's a babe?"

It was an interesting exercise, but figuring Jason out had never been Athena's strong point.

"She's been hanging around Jason a lot lately," Tracy went on cautiously.

Now that she thought about it, Athena remembered seeing Susan and Jason working at a computer terminal in lab. That wasn't unusual. Jason helped a lot of the students. But Susan was something of a hacker herself. How much help could she really need? And she had seemed awfully interested in Jason's open house project the night before, come to think of it.

"You think she's after Jason?" Athena asked.

"Do pigs fly?" Tracy replied rhetorically. "If you spent less time in cyberspace and more on solid ground, you'd see the signs. She's definitely on his case."

Susan Hunter and Jason Kane. The picture was definitely obscene. Not that Susan wasn't a nice person. Athena actually almost liked her. But she wasn't Jason's type. She was the kind of girl that would turn an honest hacker into a suit-and-tie executive. And Jason wearing a suit and tie was a sight too awful to contemplate.

As Athena said goodbye to Tracy and hurried to the computer lab, she decided she'd have to do something about Susan. But what?

The school day crawled by, and she was relieved when she finally got to the computer lab. A couple of kids were already working on projects, but the door to Mr. Madison's office was closed. She recalled that Mr. Madison had mentioned that he would be attending a computer seminar in Seattle this weekend and wouldn't be in on Friday. He hadn't mentioned who was substituting for him. Probably some geek who knew nothing about computers.

"Hey, Ath," Jason said as he brushed past her. He sat down at his terminal in the far corner of the room. Before she could reply, he was already booting up his system and starting to work.

Athena went and sat down at her own terminal and booted up Icarus. The Chicago Museum had a new online exhibit that she wanted to check out. She looked up when someone emerged from Mr. Madison's office. It was Bruce Archer! For a moment she was truly surprised. She couldn't believe that Mr. Madison would bring in someone their age to teach a class—it was kinda cool.

"What are you doing here?" Jason asked. He didn't look pleased.

"Mr. Madison asked me to substitute for him today," Bruce replied.

"You?" Jason exclaimed.

"Cool, huh?" Bruce remarked. "Would you like to see my teaching credential?"

Athena could see that Jason was about to ask

to see that very thing. "No thanks," Athena said, "We trust you." Jason frowned.

"You better stop yakking and do your work." Bruce grinned at them. Athena smiled back and watched him return to Mr. Madison's office, closing the door behind him.

"What was that all about?" Susan asked.

"You think you know a guy," Jason said and shook his head.

"Which guy?" Susan asked.

"Mr. Madison. Leaving us to the mercy of that dork," Jason replied.

"Maybe Ms. O'Malley hired Bruce," Susan suggested.

Athena stared at Jason. "What's the big deal? He isn't *that* bad."

"Never mind," Jason retorted.

Athena brought up the Internet on her computer. The blinking mailbox icon told her she had e-mail waiting. But she was too eager to visit the museum's exhibit to stop and read it. Plenty of time later.

Bruce did not emerge from the office all period. If somebody needed help, the student went to her or Jason. Athena tried not to notice how much time Susan spent with him.

Athena checked out the American Impressionists that the Chicago Museum was featuring online. The Impressionists had a slightly romantic view of big city life. They even made slums look like exciting places to live. They weren't always accurate, but they were wonderful painters. Time passed pretty quickly, and Athena was surprised when the final bell rang.

The other students picked up their stuff and left.

"Coming?" Susan asked Jason.

"Naw," he said. "I have some Cyberhut stuff to do."

"See you, then," Susan said and waited for an answer. Athena was pleased she did not get one. Jason was already deep into his programming.

Bruce emerged from the office with a file under his arm. "You feebs still here?" he asked. "I thought I heard the bell."

"You did," Jason said, "and we are."

"I have to go see Ms. O'Malley. Try not to burn the joint down," he joked as he walked out the door.

"Should we burn the joint down?" Jason asked while he and Athena watched him stroll down the hall toward the main office.

"I'd rather read my e-mail," Athena said. She moved her mouse pointer and double-clicked on the icon.

The first letter scrolled onto the screen:

Hi Athena.
This is Rebel.
Have a nice day.
Enjoy it while you can. :/x

For a signature Rebel used a creepy imp with a leering face, big hairy ears, and a lopsided squint. A feeling of dread held her. Apparently

Rebel didn't like having his cage rattled. She watched helplessly as the e-mail scrolled.

```
Hi Athena.
This is Rebel.
Have a nice day.
Enjoy it while you can. :/x
```

The same letter. He's doing to me what I did to him, Athena thought. Sending me tons of e-mail—the same stupid message over and over again.

Only Rebel wasn't content to send ten letters or even a hundred. They just kept coming. Frantically she tried to close the electronic mailbox and trash the letters before they filled up her hard disk.

```
Ah-ah-ah . . .
Athena, don't touch that mouse . . .
```

Suddenly the letters scrolled faster and faster yet till they were moving too fast to read. No matter what she did, she couldn't stop the deluge of e-mail.

"What're you doing, Ath?" Jason called to her. "The system's slowing down, like it's on overload."

Athena could see her own computer struggling under the weight of the tidal wave of data pouring into it as if a digital dam had burst. And the input was obviously affecting the whole school network.

Jason leaped from his chair and ran over to Athena. "Turn off your computer before the whole system crashes!"

Athena had been staring at her monitor, numbed by what was happening. Jason's order awoke her, and she jabbed the power button.

"I can't turn it off," she cried.

"The whole system is down," Jason said as he ran from terminal to terminal. "And it's all your fault!"

Cybersurfers

3

chapter three@cybersurfers.cybercops
chapter three@cybersurfers.cybercops
chapter three@cybersurfers.cybercops

Athena looked at Jason with big horrified eyes. Jason always felt like a sucker for those eyes. Ms. Competent Athena had never seemed as totally vulnerable and helpless as she did at that moment.

"It's OK," Jason said gently. as he contemplated the imp on her screen. "I didn't mean to go ballistic. I know this isn't *your* fault."

He was amazed at how calm he was now that the system had crashed. Nothing worse could happen. Around them all twelve computer terminals sat like helpless idiots, their umbilical data cords somehow internally broken—like so many electronic soldiers shell-shocked in a cyberwar. He and Ath would need all their wits to figure out what to do next.

"But it *is* my fault," Athena said, her voice shaking, on the verge of tears. She sounded like an overloaded computer herself. "If I hadn't sent an answer to Rebel, all those flaming messages, I—"

"OK, fine," Jason said, allowing a bit of annoyance into his voice. "So you acted a little human. You didn't overload his system, did you?"

"I guess not," Athena said, sounding unsure.

"And if you didn't answer him, he might have done this anyway, just to get your attention."

"I guess," Athena said and sighed. "I wish Mr. Madison was here." She sounded very tired, overwhelmed. Yeah, there was nothing like a flame war to wear out a person.

"Well, he's not," replied Jason. "He's off rubbing elbows with the suits in Seattle. We'll just have to fall back on Plan B."

"What's that?"

"*We* are Plan B." He grinned at her and was rewarded by a weak, uncertain smile.

Athena wiped her hand across her eyes. "OK, Mr. Spock, I'm game. What did you have in mind?"

"We'll try the easy stuff first," he said as he reached behind Athena's machine and switched it off. But when he tried to reboot the system, it was frozen. He couldn't reconnect to the network. "Whoever bombed us knew what he was doing," Jason commented, more intrigued than angry. There was nothing like a hacking problem to get the juices flowing.

"So what do we do now?" Athena asked. She was hovering over his shoulder.

Before Jason could reply, they were interrupted by an angry voice: "What is going on in here?"

Jason recognized Principal O'Malley's voice. He and Athena turned to watch her bearing down on them like an angry force of nature.

"There's been," Athena began and searched for the word, "a glitch,"

"Glitch?" Ms. O'Malley exclaimed in exasperated disbelief. She entered the room, her eyes darting from place to place as if she expected to find burglars crouching in the corners. "Glitch?" Ms. O'Malley asked again, her voice rising. "Is that what you call it when we can no longer access our attendance records or our grade database? Is that what you call it when my secretary can no longer type a simple letter? Is that the official computer word for all that? A glitch?"

"Yikes!" Athena muttered. She looked at Jason. Her face screwed up into an expression of pained wonderment.

Ms. O'Malley's announcement shocked Jason into remembering that all the computers in the school were linked up through a LAN—Local Area Network—and whatever blew out the Internet program would also overload the network's resources. Innocent victims of cyberspace crossfire, they were all sitting helplessly in the dark.

A joke about sitting in the dark came to him. How many computer programmers does it take to change a lightbulb? Computer programmers don't change lightbulbs. That's a hardware problem. Hilarious. Why did his brain bother with this stuff?

"Don't worry, Ms. O'Malley," Jason said with more assurance than he felt. "Everything is under control."

"Is that true, Athena?" Ms. O'Malley asked.

"I have faith in Jason," Athena said.

Bless her, thought Jason grateful for her support.

But Ms. O'Malley hadn't heard Athena's answer. "I've always hated computers," she said. "Electronic brutes that nobody understands."

"The sooner I get to work," Jason suggested, "the sooner we'll be up and running again." He wasn't in any mood for one of Ms. O'Malley's sermons about the evils of modern technology.

"Perhaps I can be of assistance," Bruce Archer said as he stepped up beside Ms. O'Malley.

In the excitement, Jason had forgotten all about Bruce. He knew he couldn't fix the system himself, yet the thought of allowing Bruce to help him was so unpleasant, his mind immediately rejected the idea.

"Bruce," Ms. O'Malley cried with obvious relief. She didn't quite hug him, but it was close. "Yes, you may certainly help. I believe our system can be described as down."

"Let me see," Bruce said as he pushed Jason aside and sat down in Athena's chair. He tapped a few keys, and of course nothing changed. "Tell me exactly how this happened."

Ms. O'Malley looked at Athena and Jason expectantly. Jason folded his arms and said nothing. "Athena?" Ms. O'Malley asked.

"It's a dirty job," Jason whispered to Athena. Athena told Bruce about the onslaught of letters, the crashing, the appearance of the leering imp. She was altogether less sarcastic than Jason knew he would have been.

Bruce nodded. "I see," he said every now and

again. When Athena finished, he shut down the power and rebooted the computer.

"I already tried that," Jason remarked.

"Locked up good," Bruce said, and pushed himself back from the terminal. Over his shoulder, he looked at Jason. "We're going to have to do a total reinstall of the network software."

"Mr. Madison set up the system to automatically back itself up every twenty-four hours at midnight," Athena said. "He keeps the tapes in his office. In the file cabinet."

"But it's locked," Jason added.

"He keeps the key in the top left drawer of his desk," Athena said. Bruce went into the office with Ms. O'Malley.

"Why are you helping him?" Jason whispered to Athena when they were inside.

"I'm getting our system back online," Athena whispered.

"I hate it when you're right," Jason replied.

Bruce came out of the office holding a high-density backup tape. "I'd appreciate it," he told Ms. O'Malley as she came out, "if Athena and Jason would stick around. I could use some help."

"They may stay after school to help if they so desire." Ms. O'Malley said imperiously. She glared at them. "Personally, I believe that since Athena and Jason made this mess, it is only right they help clean it up. They may use the telephone in the main office to call their parents." She turned and walked away, her footsteps clicking against the linoleum in the hall.

Jason wasn't happy with either of them being blamed for the crash, and he was even less enthusiastic about being a gofer for Bruce. "What do you say, Ath?"

"I say what do we do first?"

"First," Bruce interrupted, "you kids can thank me for saving your buns."

Athena and Jason went to the main office to call their parents. The excuse that they were fixing a computer problem for the school principal smoothed a lot of ruffled feathers.

By the time Athena and Jason got back to the computer lab, Bruce had already started the tape backup routine to restore the system to where it had been the day before.

For nearly two hours Jason and Athena sat and watched the flickering lights as the tape data replaced the corrupted information on the main server computer. It was boring, but at least Bruce wasn't around. He had run off on some mysterious errand.

"Watch closely," Bruce said when he returned. The backup was finished and he rebooted the system. This time everything seemed to work. "You feebs might learn something." He began to reinitialize the network.

Jason applauded slowly and with heavy sarcasm. "So we get the system back where it was," he said. "What's to prevent Rebel from doing the same thing again?"

"I'm a security expert, remember?" Bruce said. "I can build a firewall around anything."

"You mentioned firewalls at the open house," said Athena. "What does it mean?"

"You're not much of a hacker, are you kid?"

Bruce said, staring hard at Athena.

"She's an artist," Jason replied in her defense.

Bruce took out a software distribution disk from his shirt pocket and shoved it into the floppy disk drive. He typed in Install and pushed Enter, and the software loaded. "Firewalls are special computers and programs that isolate the heart of a vulnerable system from intruders," he explained.

"You mean like the electrified fence around the Army base near Mill Valley?" Athena asked.

"Very good," Bruce said as though they were children. "Firewalls keep *us* separated from *them*."

"Rebel breached our firewall," Jason said.

"That shows what you know," Bruce said. He flipped the circuit relays, powering up the main server computer that ran the school's network. "Rebel crashed your system, but he did it by getting in through the usual channels, not by penetrating your security." Bruce put up a hand to his mouth as if he were telling Jason a secret. "Rebel managed to bring us to our knees, but he didn't learn our secrets."

Jason watched as one system light after another flashed from red to green. "So you're going to build a bigger and better firewall?" Jason asked.

"I guess you're trainable after all," Bruce said. He pointed to the floppy disk in the disk drive. "That's what this little item is for."

Jason and Athena looked at the computer screen and saw a K-9 Corps guard dog appear in the center of the screen. It growled.

"Cute," Athena remarked.

Jason watched as Bruce typed in a set of commands that initiated the program. "Jasper the Wonder Dog is a terminate-and-stay-resident program. From now on whenever you boot up your system, ol' Jasper will be lurking in the background. He will be the school's firewall—or in this case, watchdog." Bruce chuckled. "Whenever the incoming data flow gets too heavy to handle, Jasper will shut it off. A primitive approach, but it works."

"How about telling us Jasper the Wonder Dog's password just in case we need to get into the program?" Jason asked.

"Hey, this is top secret stuff. I'll tell ol' Madison and Ms. O'Malley, but that's all."

"That's all right, Jason," Athena said. "If we don't know the password, nobody can accuse us of leaking it. If Rebel bombs the system again, we're clear."

"I like it," Jason said.

"Like it or not," Bruce said, "that's the way it's going to be." He went off to check out the school's administrative terminals, leaving Jason and Athena to do the same with the terminals in the computer lab.

"Looks like we're out of the woods," Jason said when they finished running a diagnostic program on the final terminal.

"The school may be," Athena replied as she slumped in her chair in front of her terminal. "But I don't think I am yet."

Watching her, Jason imagined what she was thinking: What was Rebel planning next?

chapter four@cybersurfers.cybercops
chapter four@cybersurfers.cybercops
chapter four@cybersurfers.cybercops

By the time Athena got home, Ralph and her parents were already in the kitchen eating dinner. In the middle of the table was a big salad and an even bigger casserole of macaroni and cheese. Both were already about half gone.

She dropped her books and her jacket in the dinning room—where her mom normally graded college English papers—and washed her hands at the kitchen sink.

Athena sat down at the table. "How's Ms. O'Malley's problem?" her mother asked as she dished food onto Athena's plate.

"Uh, we fixed it," Athena said as she dug in. Between the three of them, she, Jason, and Bruce had gotten the school's computer system back up and running. Athena thought Bruce was a first class hacker. Even Jason had been impressed.

"What was it?" Ralph asked.

How honest could she be with her family before she frightened them? It was enough that she was frightened. Still Ralph's question was reasonable and friendly. It deserved an answer. If she could think of one.

"The school's computers crashed," Athena said.

"Those things are always having problems," Mr. Bergstrom replied.

"Eventually we found out that some kid accidentally spilled chocolate milk into a keyboard," Athena lied, suddenly inspired.

Even Mr. Bergstrom had to laugh at that.

"So what did you do?" Ralph persisted.

"Not much we could do. We got a new keyboard," Athena lied. Gee, once you get started lying, it just gets worse, she thought. She decided to change the subject. "How about you guys?"

"I was home most of the day," Mrs. Bergstrom said, "and I got some strange phone calls."

"Sean Connery again?" Mr. Bergstrom asked, chuckling. "That fellow just won't give up."

"Stranger than that," Mrs. Bergstrom said, obviously baffled. She shook her head and looked at her husband with worried eyes. "I got about three calls asking me to subscribe to *Ironmonger's Monthly*."

"I never heard of that," Ralph remarked.

"Neither have I," Mrs. Bergstrom said. "And then I got six or eight calls asking me if I would sell them a subscription to some magazine that caters to people who collect antique slot machines."

"Where'd they get this number?" Ralph asked.

"That's what I asked every one of them," Mrs. Bergstrom went on. "They all got it off some Internet bulletin board."

Everyone looked at Athena, making her very uncomfortable. As far as her family was concerned, she was responsible for the operation of all computers everywhere.

"I didn't put it there," she said and laughed uncomfortably.

"Jason maybe?" Mr. Bergstrom asked.

"I don't think so," Athena said. She knew who put the number there, and it was not Jason. Apparently, it wasn't enough for Rebel to cause trouble for her. He had to cause trouble for her family, too. That was his mistake. She was still afraid of him, but now she was angry again, too. Rebel would be sorry. She didn't know how yet, or when, but he would be, she promised herself.

"Something wrong, dear?" Mrs. Bergstrom asked. "You've been so moody lately."

Angry, maybe. Frightened out of her mind, perhaps. But moody? Athena shrugged. "We had a substitute in computer lab today. He kinda threw off the usual routine."

The telephone rang. They all looked in the direction of the ring, wary as if it was the cry of a wolf.

"I'll get it," Mr. Bergstrom said. He threw down his napkin as if to challenge whoever was on the other end of the phone. He had a short fuse when it came to troublemakers. He went away, and they all ate quietly while they listened to his end of the conversation—an unintelligible grumble from the other room. Very soon Mr. Bergstrom returned after hanging up the phone harder than usual. Without speaking, he sat down and began to eat. He seemed to be deep in thought.

"Dad?" Ralph said.

"Some guy with a lot of nasty ideas looking for some adult-rated videos."

The phone rang again.

"I'll get it," Athena said.

"No you won't," Mrs. Bergstrom said. She got up and was gone even less time than her husband. When she came back she was pale and distraught.

"I've had enough of this," Mr. Bergstrom said. "I'm calling the phone company." He threw down his napkin again, and this time he was gone much longer. Athena and her family sat at the table passing around worried glances and not eating, listening to Mr. Bergstrom's voice as if it were distant cannon fire. He returned and sat down. The phone rang again, but none of them moved to answer it. Mr. Bergstrom's big fists clenched on the table. After awhile the ringing stopped.

"What do they say?" Mrs. Bergstrom asked.

Mr. Bergstrom took a deep breath. "They say that they can't do anything."

"That's pretty—" Ralph began.

"They say," Mr. Bergstrom went on, "that

because the calls were legitimately dialed, and did not threaten us in any way, they can't do a thing. If we fill out a formal complaint, they can do a little checking, but they can't do anything tonight."

"What about the postings on the Internet?" Mrs. Bergstrom asked.

"The phone company doesn't have anything to do with the Internet," Athena said.

"No," Mr. Bergstrom agreed. "The phone company is a pipeline. They usually don't monitor the information flowing over the lines."

The phone rang again.

"What if it's somebody we know?" Mrs. Bergstrom asked.

"They can get along without us tonight," Mr. Bergstrom replied grimly.

"We should turn off the ringer," Ralph said.

Mr. Bergstrom nodded, and Ralph went to do it, stopping the phone in the middle of a ring.

"Well," Mrs. Bergstrom said, changing the subject, "is everybody done eating?" They were. And for once there was little interest in dessert.

Athena took her jacket and her books upstairs. She had the feeling that every move she made was observed by enemies who surrounded the house. It was important that every maneuver be done correctly, yet she feared that not one of them would change the outcome of the battle. She dropped her stuff on the bed then switched on the light over her desk.

Athena sat down and stared with apprehension at her computer. It seemed to be staring back, spying for the enemies at her gate. The computer had once been her friend—sometimes her best friend. That she could no longer trust it made her sad and angry. After a while Athena was certain that the computer was not only watching her, it was challenging her, waiting for her to do something.

She decided she couldn't tread on eggshells for the rest of her life, afraid to answer the phone and afraid to use her computer. If she did, Rebel would win. She couldn't let that happen. Boldly, without another thought, Athena reached around and switched on her computer.

She half expected to see the leering imp, but all that came up on the screen was the familiar Windows™ logo. Was it possible that Rebel had given up so soon? After harassing her with messages, and harassing her family with phone calls both irrelevant and obscene, had he at last ridden off into the night laughing and howling like a maniac in a bad summer movie?

Still careful, Athena tentatively clicked on Icarus and used it to bring up the Internet. She contemplated the flashing mailbox icon. More messages. Athena took a deep breath as if about to plunge into cold water. The messages all looked normal enough. One was from a clerk at the Chicago Museum whom she had become friendly with. The second was from a friend in Los Angeles—another Edward Hopper fan. A third was from Jason. All normal, although Jason usually called on phone. Maybe he'd tried to get through and couldn't.

She downloaded the posting from Jason, then watched the screen with dismay as the familiar e-mail home screen shattered into many colored fractals that bloomed like a growing colony of microscopic animals. The display changed constantly, and part of Athena's mind admitted it was kind of pretty, but it was also frightening.

Wait a minute, kiddo. Maybe this was a program sent by Jason. Push any key to return to application. She touched the Return key and the fractals continued to bloom, growing continents of color. She pushed Control-Alt-Delete, which was supposed to reset everything, but the fractals continued. She turned off the computer, always the ultimate solution. But when she turned the machine back on, the fractals still crawled across the screen.

Tears welled up in Athena's eyes. She didn't want to fight any more. She just wanted everything back to normal. Not knowing what else to do, she went down the hall to call Jason.

But when she picked up the phone, instead of a dial tone, she got a flat, stiff mechanical voice: "—you would have experienced overwhelming technical and personal difficulties. Press the Control key three times and you will regain control of your computer. For now." There was a click, and the message began again. "This is just a warning from your friendly technician. Had this been a real attack, you would have experienced overwhelming technical and personal difficulties. Press the Control key three times and you will regain control of your computer. For now."

Athena listened to the complete message once more. When it started a third time she hung up and stood in the hall leaning against the cool wall with her eyes closed. If she was to believe that cocky "For now," Rebel still had other things in mind for her. If she could just talk to him, explain that she'd just been reacting to what he had done to her art—not attacking his manhood or whatever he thought she had done.

Well, why not talk to him? She had Rebel's e-mail address. Maybe if she was reasonable first he would be reasonable, too. She began carefully wording her letter as she returned to her room.

Back at her computer she thought for a moment about hitting the Control key three times. What if doing that caused the computer to blow up in her face or something? If she was stupid enough to do what Rebel suggested didn't she deserve anything she got? On the other hand, nothing she'd tried had worked, and if she didn't do it she'd never know.

She pushed the Control key three times and swallowed hard when the screen went blank. When the regular e-mail home screen came up, she let out a deep sigh. Rebel had played fair with her once. Could she make him do it again?

She was about to send a message to Rebel's e-mail address when someone knocked on the door. She turned and saw it was her father.

"Can I come in?" he asked.

"Sure. I'm just cleaning up some stuff here."

He came in and sat on the end of her bed. "Is there anything you want to tell me?"

"Tell you?"

"Like about this telephone stuff." He was sitting patiently, watching her face.

Was there? Would telling him about Rebel

help solve her problem? Would telling him lighten her heart even a little? No and no, she decided. Rebel was essentially a computer problem, and she wanted to take care of it herself. If not by herself, than with Jason's help. She might even go to Bruce, the king of the firewalls, but she did not want to involve her family. Not only was she afraid of what Rebel might do, she was afraid her father would take away her computer.

"Nothing, Dad. Why?" Athena said.

"Funny phone calls is not our only problem."

She waited, knowing he would go on.

"The bank called today. Seems the gas station's checking account is overdrawn."

"That's impossible," Athena said, astonished. "You never bounced a check in your life."

"That's what I told them. But they claim their computer says otherwise."

"Well, look," Athena said as she turned back to her computer, ready to bring up her dad's electronic checkbook.

"That's not all," Mr. Bergstrom continued. "According to USX my credit rating has gone through the basement."

"Huh?" Athena's heart started pounding.

"I thought you were watching this stuff, Athena. That's why I got you the computer—not so you could play video games with Jason."

"Look at this, Dad," Athena said, eager to show him how careful she'd been with his accounts. She brought up the electronic checkbook, and they spent almost an hour reconciling it with the paper one Mr. Bergstrom kept. Everything checked to the penny.

"I don't understand," Mr. Bergstrom said.

"Just a glitch," Athena said, cringing when she remembered Ms. O'Malley's commentary on that word.

"That glitch could put us out on the street." Her dad seemed really whipped. Maybe she wasn't doing her family a favor keeping Rebel to herself. After all, they were in this together and had a right to know what was happening. She told her dad everything—about her fear of Rebel, about her hope for Bruce—everything!

"I figured it had to be something like that," he said. "I guess there's nothing we can do tonight."

"Maybe there is," Athena said. She printed out her records, a little something her dad could take to his meeting with the bank people.

"I hope this works," he said, shaking the paper at her.

"I hope so, too, Dad."

Mr. Bergstrom stood up and went to the door, where he turned. "I'd have faith in you, Athena."

"I'm doing the best I can," she said.

"I know you are," he said with a comforting glance. He walked down the hall with the printout.

All right. If she was going to clean up this mess, she should start. She called USX and got their public relations home page—a jolly happy-talk explanation of why it was a good idea for a major corporation to gather and sell information about citizens without their knowledge or consent. Nothing useful there.

Then she typed the word *Hoover*. "Where did you get this?" Athena had asked when Jason had given the password to her months ago.

He had shrugged. "I'm not the only hacker around," he'd explained.

"Why would I want to nose around inside USX anyway?" Athena had asked.

"You never know," Jason had replied mysteriously. "Sometimes it's fun to see what the big kids are doing."

At the time she'd thought that was silly, but now she was grateful for the password.

```
***** CONNECT *****

There's the USX main screen.
What's your password?
Type it in . . . wait a microsecond . . . and it
works!
Great!
Now navigate the menus. Search for Dad's files.
There. That's the current stuff. Not good. Bad
checks. Overdrawn accounts.
Look at the old information. It's all the same.
Late payments. Defaults.
Who'd give credit to a deadbeat like that?
But it's not my dad. It's someone else. It has to
be. Two accounts must be mixed up. But there's
no way to correct the mess from here.

***** DISCONNECT *****
```

Athena was shocked all over again by what she saw as she scanned the printout of what she'd found. No wonder her dad's credit rating was in the sub-basement. The problem with the report was that none of it was true. Dad hated buying on credit, and he always paid his entire bill as quickly as he could. They'd have to dig out all their old paper receipts and canceled checks—a big dusty job Athena didn't look forward to. But she saw no other way to convince USX that they were wrong.

Once they fixed everything, what was to prevent Rebel from getting in and screwing up the data all over again? They needed one of Bruce's firewalls.

Suddenly the screenful of invoice data went blank and was immediately replaced by Rebel's leering imp.

The fun is only beginning.

Athena scowled at the screen. Depends on your idea of fun, she thought. A feeling of intense gloom settled over her.

Cybersurfers

5

chapter five@cybersurfers.cybercops
chapter five@cybersurfers.cybercops
chapter five@cybersurfers.cybercops

Jason was not quite comfortable in his skin—the result of the fallout from his afternoon at the computer lab with Bruce.

Bruce was a difficult person to be around, whether he was sucking up to the adults or knocking his peers. He'd knocked Jason so hard and so many times that when he got home Jason surfed around the Internet almost half the night just to assure himself he still knew how.

The chimes of the front doorbell awoke him Saturday morning. He waited for his dad to answer it, but the chimes kept ringing. Then Jason remembered that his dad was out of town on one of his frequent business trips. He leaped out of bed, threw on a robe and ran downstairs—his bare feet cold against the floor. When he opened the door he was surprised and embarrassed to find Susan holding a white box on which grease stains were spreading. She was wearing tight jeans, combat boots, and a denim jacket over a Nirvana T-shirt—typical high-school garb but on Susan it looked better some-how. She looked terrific, but he usually didn't talk to girls while in his jammies.

He quickly hid behind the door and poked his head around it. "Hey, Susan," he said.

"Hey, Jason," she said, grinning at him. "Did I get you up?"

"Sort of. How did you know where I live?"

"You're in the book."

"Oh, yeah." Not quite awake yet, he fought impulses to scratch his head and yawn. "What can I do for you?"

"It's what I can do for you. Can I come in?"

"Sure," Jason replied. "Give me a minute, will you?" He closed the door and ran up the stairs. In seconds he was dressed. He ran back down the stairs, stopped, took a deep breath, prepared a welcoming smile on his face, and opened the door.

She handed him the white box as she walked in appraising the house, looking around as if she'd just bought it and was thinking of turning it into a parking lot.

"Doughnuts?" Jason asked as he opened the box.

"Breakfast," Susan said. "Can you make some hot chocolate?"

"Sure." He stood in the foyer, uncertain what to do next. Somehow he'd lost control of the visit. "So, you said you could do something for me?"

"I found this really great game on the Internet," she said excitedly, "and I want to share."

"Cool," Jason said. There were hundreds of games on the Net. He could not possibly have played them all. Of course some of them weren't worth playing.

"But I can't get past the first level. I thought you could help me." She grinned. "The dough-nuts are kind of a bribe."

They had doughnuts and hot chocolate in the kitchen while she told him about the game. "It's called Sixth Column," she said.

"Great game," Jason exclaimed.

"You know it?"

"I've played it a couple of times. And I did get past the first level."

"Terrific. Where's your computer?"

"Up in my room." The thought of letting Susan into his room made Jason nervous, as if it was something he shouldn't do. He'd never felt that way with Athena—she'd been up there lots of times.

They went upstairs to Jason's room together. He hadn't expected visitors so he had to do a hurried, slap-dash job of making the bed. When he turned to Susan, he was astonished to see that she was already sitting at his computer and boot-ing it up. The computer was one of his most per-sonal possessions. That someone would use it without even asking irritated him.

"Do you always just walk in and take over?"

"Oh? Sorry," she said and leaped to her feet. "I'm kind of pushy sometimes. I take after my dad."

"That's all right," Jason said, confused by the roil of emotions Susan provoked in him. "Sit down. Let's see what you can do."

She did as he suggested, clicked on Icarus and

entered the Internet. He stood at her shoulder
and watched the Sixth Column home page come
up. Words were superimposed over a burning
outline of the United States.

***** CONNECT *****

IN THE NEAR FUTURE THE UNITED STATES HAS FALLEN INTO
THE HANDS OF INCOMPETENTS. THE COUNTRY IS NO
LONGER ABLE TO CARE FOR ITS CITIZENS—MANY OF WHOM
ARE HARASSED AND REPRESSED BY THE STRONG. THE
ARMED FORCES ARE OUT OF CONTROL, ATTACKING THE
UNITED STATES' OWN CIVILIAN POPULATION. THE COUN-
TRY IS FEEDING ON ITSELF. WE ARE THE PATRIOTS WHOSE
JOB IT IS TO SAVE THE UNITED STATES.

WE ARE THE SIXTH COLUMN.

"Cool," Jason commented. Whenever he read
this introduction he got a little shiver. These
Sixth Column guys would be a dangerous gang
of wonks if they were real, but they made a terrific game.

Susan clicked on the Play icon.

You're just outside the town of Rhapsody, somewhere in the southwestern United States.
You're the leader of a paramilitary group of
commandos intent on regaining control of the

country from the faceless enemies who now control the government.

Your mission is to seize the local army base and take control of their communications network. This will give you a pipeline into the government's global computer network.

***** INTERRUPT *****

Jason paused the game. "The trick here is to destroy the power station."

"But it's so heavily guarded," Susan said as she surveyed the army tanks surrounding the station.

"A direct attack will always be defeated," Jason hinted. "Think strategy."

***** RECONNECT *****

The army tanks are linked to the base by computers. Get into their system through the back door.

First find the back door.

There it is. Now you're in.

Now you give them false orders. Send them marching to a new drummer.

Good. You've done it. The tanks are moving away from the power station.

Now you can attack. . . .

***** DISCONNECT *****

"Wow," Susan said with satisfaction as she completed the mission to destroy the power station. "It's just like real army maneuvers."

"I guess you're right," Jason said, wondering how much Susan really knew about army maneuvers. "Well, the more real the game, the better it is. Even space battle games and magic quest games have to seem real."

She turned around and rested her chin on her hands. "You really are good at this," she said while she looked up at him with what Jason took to be a certain longing. "Think you could give me some more pointers?"

"I guess," Jason said. "Here," he went on, sitting down next to her. "Let me—" He was interrupted by the ringing of the doorbell. "Be right back," he said and ran for the door. This was amazing, Jason thought. Weeks went by without anybody coming to the door. Now two visitors on the same morning. At least he was dressed this time. He opened the door and was shocked to see Athena. "What's the matter?" Athena said.

"What do you mean?"

"You look funny," Athena said, frowning.

"I didn't sleep much. That Bruce really makes me crazy."

"He's an interesting guy," she protested. Jason frowned.

"You didn't come over here to discuss Bruce."

"No. Uh, can I come in? It's cold out here."

"Sure," Jason said, holding the door open. He was aware that Susan could come down at any minute, or that Athena might have a reason to go up. Athena wouldn't understand that he and

Susan had only been playing computer games. Still, the thought of inviting Susan down to say hi caused him to sweat big time.

"You sure seem nervous," Athena said as she passed him and entered the living room. When he joined her she was sitting in the middle of the couch with her hands in her lap, staring at the floor.

"You seem pretty nervous yourself, Ath," Jason said as he stood in front of her.

"That's what I wanted to talk to you about." When Athena had finished, Jason could hardly believe all the terrible stuff that had happened to her since they'd seen each other in school the previous afternoon—the online threat, the phone calls, the bounced checks, the trashed credit rating.

"The bad part is that it's hurting my dad even worse than it's hurting me. I flamed Rebel back when you told me not to, so I guess I have to take the heat for some of what's happened. But the Bergstroms haven't bounced a check in three generations—not since they came here from Europe. And Dad uses credit only when necessary—he's not some kind of plastic junkie. He plays fair with everybody. He never expected to deal with stuff like this, and he just doesn't know how."

Jason knew he'd been in the living room for a long time. At any moment Susan could come down. But Athena was pretty broken up about Rebel's attack on her family—he couldn't just rush her out. She was his friend, maybe his only real friend. She needed some attention right now, and he was going to give it to her, no matter how dangerous giving it might be.

"Listen, Ath," Jason said as he sat down on the couch, "I know things seem pretty bad right now, but I have a few tricks left on the old hard disk," he tapped the side of his head. "I'll find out what's going on and fix things if I can."

"What if you can't?"

"At least we'll have a better idea what we're up against," he said.

"OK, Jason. Thanks." She got up and hugged him. Jason hugged her back. It felt like the right thing to do.

She let herself out, leaving Jason on the couch, hoping that he could come up with some tricks to help Athena. At the moment he was fresh out.

"You and the lumberjack are pretty tight, huh?"

Jason looked up, surprised to see Susan leaning against the living room entryway with her arms folded. Her tone made him uncomfortable.

"If you mean Athena, then yeah, we are."

She slinked across the floor and sat down next to him. "Being tight with me can be a lot more satisfying," she said, breathing her warm, flowery breath into his face.

Susan was very cute, and sitting here like this had its own exotic charm, but Jason just plain didn't like her—not least of all because she obviously had a nasty streak, and would cut out Athena's heart in a nanosecond if she thought it would do her any good.

Suddenly he had a thought. Could she be Rebel? Susan knew enough about computers. And she might be nasty enough to give Ath trouble just for the fun of it, let alone because she thought it might somehow bring her closer to him. Maybe it was a good idea to get closer to Susan, just to find out for sure. All this went through his mind while she waited, blinking at him with her big, sea-green, Barbie-doll eyes.

"Listen, Susan," Jason said hurriedly, "I can see where being tight with you would be, uh, educational, but I don't have time right now."

"A project for the lumberjack?" she accused.

"No, uh, nothing like that," Jason stammered. "I've got to tweak the Cyberhut."

"You sure?" she asked, rubbing his arm.

"Sorry. We can get together some other time, and I'll give you more pointers on Sixth Column. I promise."

Susan nodded, gracefully rose, and walked to the door, capturing Jason's entire attention with her lithe movements. She left soon after that, abandoning Jason on the couch where he sweated and practically gasped for breath.

A few minutes later he went upstairs and sat down at his computer. He exited Sixth Column, and brought up the USX home screen. No help here. The home screen was all public relations.

***** CONNECT *****

Down . . . down . . . down . . .
You're in the USX personal database area.
Find the Bergstrom file.
There it is.

Now pull up the history. . . .

Not good.

In fact it's very, very bad. The Bergstrom in the USX file is a major credit risk.

Try to change the records.

ACCESS DENIED.

Like you thought . . . you can look, but you can't touch.

***** DISCONNECT *****

Amazing, Jason thought, as he contemplated the hash on the screen. The situation was even worse than Athena knew. She probably hadn't been able to delve as deeply as he had.

Rebel not only had his basic hacking down, he or she or it had a mean streak as well. As bad as things were for Ath's family, Jason was afraid that Rebel was just getting started.

Athena felt better after seeing Jason. She even convinced her father to try turning the phone back on. He wasn't sure it was a good idea, but he agreed. The funny thing was, instead of ringing all the time, the phone didn't ring at all. Athena picked up the receiver a few times to see if they had a dial tone, and she caught her mom doing it too. The phone seemed to be working. In its own way, the phone not ringing was even spookier than the phone ringing too much.

Athena used her computer to do her homework and was relieved not to be bothered by any sign of rudeness. Of course, she didn't log onto the Internet. But still, against all logic, she found herself being hopeful.

That lasted until Jason came over on Sunday afternoon. Mr. Bergstrom glared at him suspiciously, and then turned back to his football game on TV without saying a word.

Athena took Jason up to her room. "Well?" she demanded.

"What can I say?" Jason said. "You're cursed."

"If I am, I'm cursed by Rebel. Is that all you can tell me?"

"I was able to tap into USX's main database," Jason offered.

"Congratulations. What did you find?"

"Rebel has your dad's records so screwed up I couldn't figure out how it was done, let alone how to fix it."

"I'm doomed," Athena said.

They sat in silence for a long time. Athena felt despondent. Rebel might harass them for the rest of their lives. Downstairs, Mr. Bergstrom and Ralph shouted their approval of some wonderful football play.

"I have a terrible idea," Athena said, excited about it nonetheless.

"If it's terrible, why bother?" Jason asked.

"No, it's a good idea. You just won't like it."

"Try me."

"I can talk to Bruce," Athena said.

Jason recoiled.

"Mr. Firewall?" Jason said noncommittally. "Makes sense."

"You think I should?" she asked.

"I think you can try, if you're willing to take the abuse that will go along with any help you might get."

"Look, you might think Bruce is a jerk, but at this point I'll do anything to stop Rebel."

"All right, then," Jason said sighing. "It's your party, you can try if you want to."

Athena went to school early on Monday so she would have a chance to ask Ms. O'Malley how to get in touch with Bruce. The business cards he had so proudly given them at their first meeting had only his permanent California address.

Ms. O'Malley smiled. "I'm not surprised you've come to like him. He says that you and Jason are very bright for your age."

"Thanks," Athena said.

"You're in luck," Ms. O'Malley went on. "Bruce will be here tomorrow to help me with a little *glitch* of my own."

"Jason and I could—"

"I would rather have professional help, thank you." She glared across the room as if Athena had insulted her.

"I guess I would, too," Athena admitted. "Will you tell him I need to talk to him?"

"Of course."

The day dragged on. All Athena could think about was the troubles she and her family were having, and what Bruce Archer could do for them. More than one teacher commented angrily on her daydreaming. "Thinking about Tom Cruise, are we?" her math teacher inquired. "Or is it Brad Pitt this week?" Athena had blushed in embarrassment and anger.

When she got to computer lab, she was pleased to see Mr. Madison back in charge. He was in the corner talking to Jason.

"Glad to have you back, sir," Athena said when she walked up.

Mr. Madison nodded. "Jason tells me that Bruce Archer was your substitute."

"What a jerk," Jason said.

"I'm sure he's competent," Mr. Madison said, pursing his lips.

"Jason wanted him to show us his teaching certificate," Athena said, making them all laugh. "Anything new on the Rebel front?" Athena asked Jason when Mr. Madison had gone into his office.

"Not since yesterday. You?"

"Bruce is working on a project for Ms. O'Malley. He'll be in tomorrow."

"I can hardly wait."

Athena shrugged. "Maybe he can help."

She worked on the lesson for the week. It was a simple BASIC programming assignment, but her final code, while it did the job, was sloppy. Her mind was elsewhere, and when the bell rang she was more than ready to go home. Tracy was waiting for her on their usual corner.

"So, Ath, make any good obscene phone calls lately?" Tracy asked as they crossed the street.

"Excuse me?"

"I tried calling you a bunch of times over the weekend. The phone just rang and rang."

"We turned off the phone," Athena said, feeling guilty.

"And then," Tracy continued, smirking, "I tried again and got this really weird message involving private body parts and a lot of heavy breathing."

"Oh?" This was new.

"Yeah. At first I thought I got the wrong number, but I got the same slobbering guy three times in a row. Some of the stuff he suggested seemed physically impossible," Tracy giggled.

"Hmm."

"Any ideas?" Tracy looked at her, eyebrows up in question.

"Yeah. Listen, Tracy, I'm really sorry, but I didn't do it."

"I didn't think you—"

"Well, actually, I *did* do it."

"You did?" Tracy seemed more intrigued than horrified.

"A guy flamed me on the Internet, see, and I made the mistake of flaming him back. Evidently, he's some kind of psycho."

"What's flaming?"

"Sending an insulting message."

"Uh huh. So you flamed this psycho. How did he get control of your telephone?"

Athena shook her head. "It's amazing what you can do if you know the right codes and passwords."

"Hacking," Tracy said simply. "You told me about that."

"This guy is even better at it than Jason, and lots meaner. The dirty phone messages are a new wrinkle. But that's not all. We got our phone bill this morning and on it were several calls to Zanzibar."

"Zanzibar?"

"It's a tiny island off the coast of Tanzania!" Athena cried, impatiently. "Zanzibar's in Africa, Tracy. I don't know anybody in Africa!"

"Calm down, Ath."

"Sorry," Athena said, trying to get control of herself. "But you don't know what it's like. Dad's credit rating is sinking like a stone, and his checks are bouncing."

"Your dad's checks are bouncing?" Tracy asked with amazement.

"I'm telling you, this Rebel guy is good."

"Rebel's the psycho you flamed?"

Athena nodded. She was miserable. "Jason says I'm cursed."

"Always looking on the bright side. What about me?"

"What about you?" Athena asked.

"I told you I'm house-sitting for the Hendersons," Tracy reminded her.

"Yeah. Sounds like a great gig."

"Sure it's a great gig," Tracy said, "but the Henderson farm is out in Mill Valley."

"So? Do you need a ride or what?" Athena was getting impatient with this meaningless chitchat.

"Don't you see? Mill Valley is next door to where the Army is holding their maneuvers."

"Don't worry," Athena said. "They'll stay in their part of the valley."

"I hope so," Tracy replied.

Athena was the one with the problem, but she spent the rest of their walk convincing Tracy that the Army knew what it was doing—after all, they were computerized—and she had nothing to fear. When Athena got home, her mom was in the dining room correcting English papers. The house smelled wonderful.

"Anything new?" Athena asked.

"All quiet on the western front," Mrs. Bergstrom said. "How about with you? Any luck with that Bruce fellow?"

"He'll be at school tomorrow. I'll talk to him then. What's that great smell?"

"Tri-tip roast. I'm stewing it in wine."

At least Athena still had an appetite.

Dinner was as delicious as it smelled, but the meal was still unpleasant. Mr. Bergstrom spoke only in grunts, and that was only when someone asked him a direct question. He was entirely preoccupied and refused to tell anybody what about. "You'll find out soon enough," he said. To Athena it sounded like a warning.

They finished eating, and Athena helped Ralph clear the table. It was unusual for everybody to stick around when dinner was over, but tonight nobody left. Athena knew her father had something to say, and evidently the others did, too. Mr. Bergstrom stood up and looked at them, downcast and tired.

"What is it, dear?" Mrs. Bergstrom asked.

"Bad news. My credit cards are all maxed out, and the bank tells me that they are no longer honoring my checks."

"Dad, I—" Athena began.

"I'm not blaming anybody. There are bad people in the world, and sometimes we run afoul of them. The point is, we have to do something about this Rebel soon or we'll be sucking sidewalk."

"It's just a glitch, Dad," Athena explained. "A computer error."

"Can you fix it?" Ralph asked.

"I'm working on it."

"I wish you'd work a little faster, Athena," her

father said. "Right now the only thing keeping this family afloat is the Army. Those vehicles of theirs use a lot of gasoline from my station."

Athena scrunched down into herself and stared at the pattern in the Formica-topped table. She had seen homeless people on TV, and she was terrified that her family would soon join their ranks. Rebel did this, but it was all her fault. If she had never answered him, never flamed him back . . .

But wait a minute. Jason had said Rebel might have done this anyway, just because he could. She was the victim here. She didn't ask this Rebel to ruin her family. That was his idea.

"I'm supposed to see that Bruce guy at school tomorrow," Athena said. "He's an expert on computer security."

"More computers," Mr. Bergstrom said with disgust.

"Computers caused our problem," Athena admitted, "but they can solve our problem, too."

"I hope you're right."

They sat at the table staring at each other until the front doorbell rang.

"Who could that be at this hour?" Mr. Bergstrom asked.

"Probably somebody selling insurance," said Athena's mom.

"I'm not buying," Mr. Bergstrom said as he rose and headed for the front door. He came back in a moment with two policemen. Everybody looked grim. Athena could not imagine what the problem might be. Could anything be worse than what they'd been discussing?

"What is it?" Mrs. Bergstrom asked.

"These gentlemen," Mr. Bergstrom said, "are here to arrest Ralph—for armed robbery."

chapter seven@cybersurfers.cybercops
chapter seven@cybersurfers.cybercops

Jason was doing this week's computer lab assignment with the half of his brain that was awake. Half a brain was all it took, of course, but he still thought maybe he ought to stop playing Sixth Column all night.

Susan had been eyeing him since she came in, making Jason a little nervous. He was playing a delicate game. On the one hand he did not want to actually experience Susan's version of a relationship. He suspected that going around with Susan could be pretty hard on a guy. On the other hand, he didn't want to discourage her entirely. After all, she was his number one suspect—to be truthful, his only suspect—for Rebel.

When Athena came into the computer lab, she looked like a hunted animal. Her eyes had dark smudges under them, and she glanced around nervously. She lifted a hand and gnawed briefly on a fingernail.

"What a night," she said.

"Rebel?"

"Yeah. I think so. The police came to the house last night and arrested Ralph for armed robbery."

"Your brother, Ralph?" Jason would not have been more astonished if Athena claimed that she herself had been arrested.

"Yep. My brother, Ralph. The guy who took back a candy bar that had been accidentally bagged with his groceries. The guy who'll fix your car for less than the estimate if he can. That Ralph. Public enemy number one."

"You're babbling, Ath. What happened?"

"Well, the police found out that if you arrest one Bergstrom, you arrest them all. My parents and I went with Ralph to the police station and stayed there all night trying to straighten this whole thing out. Ralph was in a holding cell this whole time, you understand. Somehow, he had acquired a list of priors—everything from stealing hubcaps to selling dope."

"This is a small town. The police must know Ralph's reputation."

"Sure they do. Some of them come into my dad's gas station to have their cars fixed. They were as surprised as anybody. But Ralph had this record. They had to throw him in the can."

"Sheesh!" Jason was astounded.

"The situation began to turn around when someone finally realized that the robberies happened in Cincinnati."

"Ohio?"

"Using car repair orders, we could prove that Ralph was in Fort Benson when those crimes were supposedly committed in Cincinnati. So

hey let him go—a little embarrassed to have col-
ared him at all, I think."

"Duh," Jason remarked. "I hope they're look-
ng around to see if their system has been
reached."

"They said they would. I offered to help, but
hey wouldn't let me."

"Of course not. They wouldn't want to be
hown up by a high school kid," Jason said.
'What time did you get to bed?"

"About four, I think."

Jason had gotten to bed about four himself,
ut he didn't believe this was a good time to
nention he'd been up all night playing video
games. He frowned. "Rebel doesn't strike me as
he kind of guy who would make that Cincinnati
nistake."

"He doesn't, does he? Which means he did it
n purpose. Which means this whole arrest busi-
ess was just more harassment. I wish I under-
tood what was going on. I wish I could see the
nd of it." She folded her arms on the desk next
o Jason's computer and put her head down.

Jason looked at her helplessly. He'd done all
e could do to help her with his computer. All
ould do now was be her friend. Tentatively, he
atted her shoulder.

Susan strolled over, an expression of concern
n her face. "Poor dear," she said. "No date for
he prom?"

Athena lifted her head and looked at Susan
rom baleful, red eyes. Jason guessed Athena had
een crying.

"If that was my biggest problem," Athena

said, "I would be delighted." Her voice quivered a little.

"What can we do for you, Susan?" Jason asked as pleasantly as he could.

"I thought this might be a good time for you to give me those pointers on Sixth Column."

This obviously wasn't a good time, Jason thought, which was probably why Susan had asked. She was paying him back for rejecting her the other day.

"Sure," Jason said, and stood up.

"But Jason," Athena said, sounding desperate, "I thought we would talk about—well, you know—my problem."

Jason couldn't very well tell Athena that Susan was his main suspect, not while Susan was standing right there. Besides, if Susan wasn't Rebel he would only be giving Athena false hope. If he wanted to help Ath, only one decision was possible. He could explain later if she didn't kill him first. "I gotta go, Ath," Jason said as he got up.

Athena got to her feet. "No need," she said angrily. "I have an appointment myself. Have a good time." She picked up her stuff and marched to the other side of the room.

Watching her go tore Jason's heart out. But he smiled at Susan. "Let me show you the next level of the game. That's where it gets really interesting."

Susan smiled triumphantly and sat down next to Jason at his computer.

```
***** CONNECT *****
You have taken control of the army base at
Rhapsody.
    Your mission now is to use their computer access
to gain entry into the main defense system net-
work, spread false information throughout the net-
work . . . then overload and crash the system. . . .

***** INTERRUPT *****
```

This was fun because it used logic and strate-
y rather than the usual crash and burn methods
son found in most games.

While he showed Susan how to run tactics and
ealth on Sixth Column, Jason watched Athena
ut of the corner of his eye to make sure she was
K. She was angry, that was for sure. Well, better
ngry than crying.

Then Bruce came in and sat down next to
thena. Jason had expected him in today, but the
uy still gave him a pain. He was using that self-
tisfied smile on her. Athena caught Jason look-
g at her, and gave him the evil eye before once
gain concentrating on what Bruce was saying.

Jason smiled at Susan, but felt dead inside.
ruce putting the make on Athena was bad
ough. But if he was wrong about Susan, he
ay have lost his best friend for nothing.

Furious, Athena grabbed her stuff and hurried to the opposite side of the room. All these months she'd misjudged Jason. She had thought that above all, no matter what, he'd be there for her when she needed him. She was as angry at herself for being so gullible as she was at him for being such a jerk. She thought they were friends, a team. Now it turned out that he would shut her down at the first sign of a pretty face and a great body. Men were all alike! They were all beasts running entirely on their glands. She didn't know why women bothered sharing the planet with them!

While Athena sat there deciding whether to cry or draw blood, arranging and rearranging her stuff, Bruce had come in and sat down beside her. At least he was nice to her. Athena wanted to be alone, but even in her overwrought state she knew he wasn't responsible for Jason's actions. Besides, she needed Bruce, really needed him.

"Hey, Bruce."

"Hey, Athena. Spat with the boyfriend?"

"He's not my boyfriend," Athena said a bit too loudly. The other kids looked at her, including Jason. She shot him her most evil look and turned to smile at Bruce.

"So, Bruce, thanks for coming. I'm having kind of a computer problem."

"What kind of problem?"

"I've got this hacker angry at me. He calls himself Rebel, and he's attacking me and my family through the Internet."

"The same guy who crashed the school's network?" he asked.

Athena nodded. "That's Rebel."

"Sounds like a cybermaniac to me." Athena saw his eyes light up, kind of like Jason's did when he had to meet a serious computer challenge. "Fire up your Internet gateway, and let's have a look."

Athena double-clicked on Icarus and fell into the Internet. Her mail icon was blinking, and she stared at it dully. I don't want to deal with this, she thought.

"You have mail," Bruce said, pointing out the obvious. His face was practically cheek to cheek with to hers. She tried not to notice.

"It's probably from Rebel," Athena said.

"All the better. Let's have a look."

He was probably right. She clicked on the icon, and saw a couple of messages, all from people she knew. It didn't matter. Last time a message that was supposed to be from Jason had really been from Rebel.

"Don't worry about a thing, honey," Bruce

said, starting to sound a little oily to Athena. "I'm here now."

She was going to ask him not to call her honey, but decided against it. This guy probably thought all women were accessories to his own life. Changing him would take more than constant whining from a high school girl.

Athena chose a message at random, and sure enough, it was from Rebel. And he was even more obnoxious than usual.

YOU DOOFS, WIMPS, AND WANNABES MAKE ME SICK. STAND UP FOR YOUR RIGHTS OR DIE WITH THE DOGS!

"He's a real cyberdude, isn't he?" Bruce commented appreciatively.

"That's not the worst of it," Athena said. "These messages are spreading around to the other computers in school."

"OK, I get the idea," Bruce said, holding up his hands. "But I can't fix anything using this Tinker Toy set up of yours. I'd say the best thing you can do right now is shut down your Internet program and meet me at my office after school." He jotted down the address.

"Thanks," Athena said as Bruce turned and strolled out of the room. She looked over at Jason. He was still embroiled with Susan. Athena sighed. No sense asking him to go with me, she thought. I'm on my own.

Bruce had suggested she stay off the Internet

till Rebel was out of the picture, and that was probably the wise thing to do. But looking at the latest message again, she decided it was not at all like the screeds Rebel had sent before. Every earlier message had been directed at her personally. This one was just sort of a general rant. Had Rebel changed his style, or was the message not from Rebel at all? Athena shook her head. Rebel was not the only sick person out there. OK, so she was curious. Maybe that meant she was a little sick too.

OK you nasty little creep . . . let's see where you live . . .

**** CONNECT ****

You know how to use the Internet's automated mailservers to find someone's home address.

But—surprise! You don't have to dip into your magic bag of cybertricks. The note isn't from Rebel. It's from a place called Sixth Column.

But what's Sixth Column? Log in as a guest and see what they're about. Paramilitary dudes . . . creepy. Jump over to ONLINE NEWS SERVICES. Search for PARAMILITARY. Double-click on the hypertext. An article appears on the screen:

DO PARAMILITARY ORGANIZATIONS THREATEN OUR NATIONAL SECURITY?

In dozens of states, loosely organized paramilitary groups are signing up new members, stockpiling

---

weapons, and preparing for the worst. They call themselves "citizen militias" and are the armed, militarized edge of a vocal minority of disgruntled men and women who feel abandoned by the government and have a distrust for those in power that goes far beyond typical voter anger. "The low-life scum that are supposedly representing us in Washington, D.C. don't care about the people back home anymore," said one member who agreed to be interviewed anonymously.

The militias believe that foreign powers are working within the United Nations on secret treaties to seize power from the United States. They fear that America will be subsumed into "one big, fuzzy, warm planet where nobody has any borders," and allege that the government is going to import Chinese and Russian soldiers to replace local police.

Such wild allegations have proved to be effective in grabbing the attention of the disaffected and recruiting them into militias. And to prepare themselves for this coming invasion, militia members play war games in the woods to be ready in case of an armed conflict.

The militia movement may be the first national movement organized on the Internet. Militias communicate with one another through linked computer bulletin boards and by postings in the newsgroups.

Critics of the militias fear they could turn into something more menacing, saying that some of the people emerging as militia leaders have ties with hate-mongering groups. The greatest fear is not armed revolution, but something far more dangerous—a high-tech rebellion that takes place in cyberspace. . . .

Yikes! Jump back to Sixth Column's home page. They have an honor roll of the best and brightest of these paramilitary cyberheads.
   Stop! That name near the top of the list. It's . . . Jason Kane?

***** DISCONNECT *****

Athena couldn't believe it! First she finds out that Jason is just another shallow guy, and now she discovers that he's mixed up with these paramilitary wonks. She tried to picture Jason creeping through the forest with a high-powered rifle ready to blast anything that moved. These dudes bomb buildings and want to take over the government. And Jason was one of them! Athena spent the rest of the afternoon lost in her computer art, letting it drain the fear and rage.

"Oh, Athena, are you still here?" Mr. Madison exclaimed as he came out of his office with a three-ring binder under his arm. Athena jerked back from her computer screen and looked around the room. It was deserted except for the two of them. "Where is everybody?"

"Gone home. Didn't you hear the bell ring?"

She hadn't. Looking at the clock, Athena saw that if she hurried, she could still keep her appointment with Bruce.

"Thanks, Mr. Madison. Gotta go. See you tomorrow." She ran down the hall, out of the building, and down to the bus stop.

Before the bus came Athena had time to wonder if Jason was alone, or was lollygagging around somewhere with Susan. Maybe Susan was a militia member, too. She decided not to burn any more brain cells worrying about it, but thoughts of Jason continued to intrude until the bus came a few minutes later and took her to the Benson Heights Industrial Park at the other end of town.

The Benson Heights Industrial Park was a complex of warehouses, office buildings, and machine shops in a setting of trees and wide lawns. Athena approved of somebody's attempt to beautify what could have been a real urban eyesore, but there was no way to disguise the industrial nature of the place.

The grounds were enormous, with twisting paths among the trees and many wide streets along which trucks boomed. Athena was lost until she came upon a map on a pedestal. After referring to it, she found the offices of Lock-Me-Tight Systems easily.

At the end of a long hallway smelling of cleaners she walked into a waiting room no larger than her own bedroom at home. The walls were decorated with old locks and keys in shadow boxes, and with framed advertisements for security software. A few armchairs and a couch stood against the walls. More than anything, the place looked like a doctor's office.

"Bruce?" Athena called out.

"Have a seat," Bruce said. His voice seemed to come from nowhere, then Athena saw a squawk box in a corner of the ceiling.

"I hope I'm not late," Athena said as she sat down in one of the chairs.

"Chill baby," Bruce said. "I'll be out in a minute."

Chill baby? Who did this guy think he was? Athena sat there without even a magazine to look at. The whole set up seemed designed to make visitors ill at ease. As far as Athena was concerned, it was working.

A door opened and Bruce leaned into the room. "You can come on in, honey." He lead her across a short hallway to his office. It was smaller than the waiting room and was crammed with stuff—filing cabinets, a drafting table, a couple of computers, and bookshelf tight with computer books. All horizontal surfaces were piled high with computer print-outs. On one wall was a map of the United States stuck all over with colored pins. On another was a flow chart. Over the computer hung a *Babylon 5* poster.

"What do you do in here?" Athena asked, marveling at the mess.

"I'm in charge of computer security for USX," Bruce said while he watched a couple of space ships float across his monitor screen.

"This is USX?" Athena cried, astonished.

"Of course not. Their offices are miles away behind barbed wire, stone walls, laser trip wires, pressure plates, cameras, and electric eyes. A cat couldn't get in there without security clearance."

"Rebel got in and screwed up my dad's credit record," she reminded him.

"It happens," Bruce said and shrugged. "USX keeps the biggest credit database in the country."

"It doesn't just *happen*." Her eyes narrowed as she glared at him accusingly. "Rebel had to get past all your famous firewalls."

Bruce spun around in his chair to face her. "Listen, honey," he said angrily, "I'm damn good at what I do, but nobody can write a perfect security program. Anything I can hack together, some other guy—like your Rebel, for instance—can crack apart. That's why I'm always trying to break into my own system, to close the holes before the bad guys find them."

Athena was about to remark that it looked as if Rebel had found one of those holes first, but she needed Bruce's help to find and stop Rebel. He was her only hope. Time to play sweet. "So can you go in through the same hole Rebel used and put everything back the way it was?" she asked instead. "Can you make sure he can't change the data again?"

"Oh, he won't get in again—not the same way, anyhow. I made sure of that. But I can't just stomp into the USX database and begin crunching numbers. You want me to get fired?"

"Well—"

"What I can do for you is write an official memo to my boss at USX, and ask her to check all their backups, see if they match the info in the main database."

Athena was disappointed. Bruce's talk had been so big, she'd expected him to wave a magic wand and immediately fix everything. The idea of waiting for some glorified cyberclerk to check backups was not very satisfying.

While she was still figuring out what to say, the phone rang. "I have to get that," Bruce said as he stood up. "Do your nails or something till I get back." He went out of the room and closed the door. Spaceships continued to drift across the monitor. Bruce Archer was really becoming an infuriating person. Athena had never in her life done her nails, and she didn't like the implication that it was all she could do with her time.

Athena wandered around the room, looking at this and that, picking up papers and putting them down. Sticking out from under a stack of fanfold printouts was a U.S. Geographical Survey topographical map. Sometimes her dad bought one of these when the family went camping in unfamiliar territory. Thousands of these maps existed; you could get one for anywhere in the country. They were blotchy green, brown, and blue things that showed ground elevation and the nature of the terrain, almost foot by foot. This one was of Mill Valley.

The word SNAFU was carefully printed across the top. Athena hurriedly scribbled down the word on a scrap of paper and shoved it into her jeans pocket. Then she noticed a file folder stuck in a corner of the table next to the map. The label read *Sixth Column*. She was about to look in the folder when Bruce returned.

He smiled at her in a friendly way that indicated he wanted something. "Business," he explained. "I'm sorry, but I have another visitor."

"I guess I better be going, then," Athena said. Neither of them moved.

"Thanks for coming in," Bruce said as he hustled her across the hallway and through the waiting room. "I'll send that memo right away."

"Thanks."

"'Bye," he said as he closed the door behind her. She stood in the public hallway, knowing that she'd just been given the bum's rush and wondering why. She didn't buy that story about "business." She might have if Bruce had remained his usual offensive self, but the politeness made her suspicious.

Outside the Lock-Me-Tight Systems' office building she stood around for a minute, then went to sit on a knob of grass behind a tree. From that position she had a clear view of the building's main entrance. She wanted to see who was coming over on "business."

Sunset was approaching and the temperature was dropping. Athena pulled her jacket around her more tightly against the cold, and saw with satisfaction that the whole complex was well-lit—she wouldn't have trouble spotting anybody who came up the walk.

Forty-five minutes later she finally saw someone. It took a moment for her to recognize who it was, and even then she had trouble believing her eyes. It was Susan!

Did Susan have something going with Bruce

even while she had her eye on Jason? Athena thought not. Susan wasn't the kind of girl who would respond well to the treatment Bruce habitually dished out, not without having a good reason. If she and Bruce had a connection, it was not social.

Athena didn't know for sure that their meeting had anything to do with Rebel or even with Sixth Column, but she wouldn't be surprised if it did. Deep in thought, Athena got up and walked slowly down the path to the bus stop. She didn't know exactly what Bruce and Susan were conspiring about, but she knew they had to be stopped.

Cybersurfers

9

chapter nine@cybersurfers.cybercops
chapter nine@cybersurfers.cybercops
chapter nine@cybersurfers.cybercops

When the end-of-school bell rang Jason glanced over at Athena and saw that she was so engrossed in what she was doing that she didn't even look up. He longed to have a closer look at her screen and to help her if he could, but he had to stay with Susan. It was a dirty job, but he was the only one who could do it.

After school, Jason hung around with Susan most of the afternoon, eating a few burgers, playing Sixth Column, necking a little. It was even fun, but he didn't learn anything new. Susan was a techno-riot grrl with a love for military games. Aside from her aggressively interesting ideas about dating, her only other relevant characteristic was that she was jealous of Athena and the close relationship she had with Jason. He was still on the fence about whether she was Rebel or not.

Because he had blown the afternoon with Susan, Jason had to go to school early the next morning to work on the Cyberhut program. He was well into the debugging phase, but the program wasn't working right yet. Of course, if he hadn't been with Susan he probably wouldn't have forgotten his software at school and he could have slept an extra hour, but he had and he did, so here he was.

He'd been working for a while when he heard two people arguing in Mr. Madison's office. Their voices were loud—he didn't have to eavesdrop. Soon he stopped typing and took an active interest in what was being said.

"I understand your concerns, Ms. O'Malley," Mr. Madison said, "but we can't shut down Fort Benson High School's gateway to the Internet just because someone is misusing it."

"We can't allow our children to be exposed to hatred and filth," Ms. O'Malley replied.

"Of course not. But we live in the real world. I'm not sure that we are doing the kids a service by turning our backs on it entirely."

"Are you suggesting that we use these messages as some sort of lesson?" Ms. O'Malley sounded horrified.

"Not a bad idea. Did you ever read Mark Twain's *The Man That Corrupted Hadleyburg*? Twain's contention was that untested virtue is the weakest kind, and I agree with him."

As the argument continued, Jason was drawn across the room to Mr. Madison's doorway. He listened for as long as he could stand it, then burst into Mr. Madison's office. Mr. Madison was sitting at his desk, and Ms. O'Malley was sitting in the visitor's chair. They looked at him with wide eyes and comically shocked expressions.

"Can we help you, Jason?" Mr. Madison said finally.

Jason felt embarrassed now that he was in the office. He shuffled his feet and looked at the floor, smiling like a fool. He wished he were anywhere else. "I, er, I just wanted to say that I agree with Mr. Madison. You can't solve a problem by pretending it isn't there. The Internet is a good thing. We can't let this Rebel jerk—whoever he is—take it away from us."

"Thank you for eavesdropping and then interrupting us with your philosophies on life, Jason," Ms. O'Malley said. "I'm sure—"

"Jason's right," Mr. Madison said. "We can't give Rebel the deciding vote."

Jason watched Ms. O'Malley's face harden while she considered that. He had the strong feeling she would still shut them down.

"Very well, then," she said, surprising him. "You technical people must solve this problem soon, or the question will be taken from my hands."

"The board of education?" Mr. Madison asked.

"Precisely." She set a card down on his desk. "If you need help, please feel free to call my nephew, Bruce Archer, at Lock-Me-Tight Systems."

"Thank you," Mr. Madison said. As Ms. O'Malley turned to the door, he winked at Jason. After Ms. O'Malley was gone, they spoke for a few minutes about the Internet, and how Jason was doing with the Cyberhut. Then they both went back to work.

"I thought you might be here, you—" Athena cried as she lunged across the room at him.

"Cool down, Ath!" Jason cried. "What's the rumpus?"

"I'll give you rumpus," Athena said angrily as she shook her finger at him.

"If it's about Susan, I can explain."

"Susan's only the beginning. What about Sixth Column?" She had him wedged against the wall now, and was shouting into his face.

"Sixth Column?" Jason asked, totally confused. "It's a great game?" he offered.

"Game?" Athena cried. "Game?" she repeated, sagging a little.

"Sure. Sixth Column is a military game on the Internet. I'll show you if you let me off the wall."

Athena moved her lips around, lowered her eyes and backed away. "Go ahead," she said and crossed her arms.

Jason went online and logged into Sixth Column. He showed her the home page, the first level of play. And, with a bit of pride, he showed her the list of big winners which included him. "See?" he said. "It's just a game."

Athena nodded. "Try this," she said, handing him a scrap of paper she pulled from her pocket.

"What is it?"

"I'm not sure. I found it in Bruce Archer's office."

"Mr. Firewall himself? Did he help you with Rebel?"

"Not as much as I would have liked. I think this Sixth Column business is a bigger deal—a much bigger deal than any *game*." She glanced at the paper. "Do you know what SNAFU means?"

"It's military," Jason said. "It means Situation Normal, All Fouled Up."

"Hmm. I was hoping it was some kind of code."

"Maybe it is. Let's find out."

```
***** CONNECT *****

OK. This is just a game . . . isn't it?
What if it's not?
Get into the Sysop section.
Try SNAFU as a password. Hmm . . . we're into
. . . some place, like a staging area for a military
operation. Looks real . . . awfully real . . . too
real.
    Those documents. They look like official U.S.
Army stuff. Download them for a later read.
    Now the maps. Check them out.
This one appears to be . . . Mill Valley?


***** DISCONNECT *****
```

"It all looks pretty convincing, doesn't it?" Athena asked.

"A good game has to look real," Jason said, though the truth was, he was no longer convinced that Sixth Column was entirely a game. "But they did seem to go a little overboard on the detail. For one thing, that's a real map of Mill Valley." He thought for a long moment. "I think Bruce is into something really terrible. What if he is somehow connected to the Army being on maneuvers?"

"Not just Bruce," Athena stated.

"Who else?"

"I saw him meet with Susan."

Jason stared at Athena with disbelief. "I thought she was just Rebel," he said.

"Why would *she* be Rebel?" Athena asked, her eyes wide with surprise.

"It was just a theory. First, she really hates you because you get along so well with me. Second, she's quite a techno-grrl."

Athena was silent for a moment. "Is that why you were hanging around with Susan, because you thought she might be Rebel?"

"Sure. What did you think?" He knew very well what Athena thought, but he just wanted to hear her say it.

She didn't. But she did hug him. "Whatever it was," she said into his shoulder, "I guess I was wrong."

Jason hugged her back. Susan had her undeniable charms, but hugging Athena felt right. That didn't mean he wanted to do it all day, of course. What if somebody saw?

"What do we do about Sixth Column?" Athena asked as Jason pulled away.

"We could call the police," Jason suggested.

"Oh, sure," Athena said. "They'll go over to Bruce's office and he'll have some totally tidy explanation for everything. Suddenly we're just a couple of paranoid kids."

"And so . . . " Jason said, not liking the direction the conversation was headed.

"And so," Athena said, "we have to catch him with his hand in the cookie jar. I want to present him to the police tied up in a pretty pink bow."

chapter ten@cybersurfers.cybercops
chapter ten@cybersurfers.cybercops
chapter ten@cybersurfers.cybercops

Because Jason was more familiar with military stuff, he volunteered to read the documents they'd pulled out of the secret Sixth Column area. He promised to let Athena know immediately if he found anything suspicious.

At the end of the day Athena emerged from the school building hunting for Tracy. Her way was blocked by a bunch of the senior boys pushing each other around, making Three Stooges noises, and generally acting like idiots. This was not unusual, and since making peace with Jason Athena could even sort of see the humor in their antics. She went around them and rushed over to where Tracy was waiting for her on the corner.

"So you and Jason are a couple again?" Tracy asked as they set out for home.

"We were never a *couple*," Athena responded patiently. Would she have to explain for the rest of her life? "We're just speaking again."

"Whatever."

While they walked, Athena wondered if she

should bring up the whole business about Mill Valley. It might alarm Tracy, and Athena wasn't sure Tracy needed alarming because she wasn't sure exactly what Bruce and Sixth Column had in mind. It was possible they were just playing a complicated military game. Even so, Athena would feel better if Tracy grabbed the Henderson's cats and just left the farmhouse.

"I had some visitors out at the Henderson place," Tracy said when they reached the other side of the street. Athena could see she was doing her best to suppress a smile.

"Oh?"

"Yeah," she went on excitedly, "a couple of Army guys came by to explain about their objectives in Mill Valley. They were way cute."

"Objectives?" Athena asked, leading Tracy on. If she was lucky, Tracy would talk herself into moving out.

"Yeah. They talked about how they were going to be tearing around in tanks and jeeps in the area. They didn't want me to be afraid of all the noise."

"So, you're not worried about them shelling the wrong place?"

"No way. They showed me how they had all the coordinates worked out on their mobile computers. The coordinates come directly from Satcom, a bunch of orbiting space satellites that tell you exactly where you are—anywhere on the planet. They assured me that shelling the wrong place was not even remotely possible."

Athena nodded, but she wondered what would happen if they got their coordinates from somewhere other than the satellite. Would the average soldier on the street know the difference?

"I'll tell you what really scares me," Tracy said, interrupting Athena's thoughts as she hopped on one foot through the squares of a hopscotch court that some kid had drawn on the sidewalk in chalk. "What really scares me is all the obnoxious stuff that's been coming into the school over the Internet."

"How did you know about that?"

Tracy looked at her with a sarcastic tilt to her mouth. "Everybody knows. The school is hip deep in talk."

"It scares me too," Athena admitted. She shook her head. "It's amazing. Any time humans get together, somebody has to be the jerk."

"We ought to just shut it down."

"What? The Internet?" Athena couldn't believe what she was hearing.

"Sure. Then those jerks will have no place to play."

"Then we can shut down parks because of the muggers and schools because of the juvenile delinquents. We can close the libraries because people steal books, and declare war on walls because of the graffiti."

"You're exaggerating," Tracy said.

"No, I'm not. You can't tear down civilization just to prevent the jerks from living in it. You have to weed out the jerks and get rid of them."

"And how do we do that?"

Athena shrugged. "If I knew that I'd write a best seller." If I knew that, Athena thought, Rebel would already be chained to a dungeon wall somewhere, losing weight on a bread and water diet. "Call me tonight . . . if you're not too busy with your new soldier boys," Athena teased.

"I can't," Tracy replied with a guilty expression. "Don't tell anyone, but I forgot to send in the check for the phone bill the Hendersons left for me. The line's going to be disconnected for a while."

They parted at their usual corner, and Athena went on alone. Thoughts of Rebel and of Sixth Column swirled unpleasantly in her head, not leading anywhere. It seemed that she'd done all she could so far. At the moment her only course of action was to wait to hear from Jason.

When Athena got home she was surprised to find her parents in the living room laughing and holding glasses of wine—not things she would have expected if the family was about to be thrown into the street.

"What's happening?" Athena asked as she entered the living room.

"USX called," Mrs. Bergstrom said. "They told us that they discovered the glitch that caused all the trouble and fixed it. Our credit rating is once again triple-A, and your father's checks no longer bounce."

"That's great," Athena cried. "I guess I owe Bruce a big thank you."

"So do I," Mr. Bergstrom said. "You should have heard those suckers apologize." He chuckled. "It was great. Thanks for your help, Athena."

"My pleasure, Dad. What about the phone company?"

"They called, too," Mrs. Bergstrom said. "And I haven't had one strange phone call all day. Except from your Aunt Edith, of course."

"Of course," Mr. Bergstrom said.

They all laughed.

"Where's Ralph?"

"Holding down the fort at the gas station," Mr. Bergstrom said. "He'll be home soon."

"Great. I'm starved." Athena went upstairs feeling better than she had in days. She dug out the business card Bruce had given her and turned on her computer. She was going to send him a nice thank-you letter by e-mail. But when she got into the Internet, instead of seeing the home page she'd expected, she was confronted by a vase full of beautiful roses and carnations. An inscription filled one corner of the screen. It read:

> Thanks for the help, sweetie.
> I learned everything I needed to know.

It was signed with a small version of Rebel's leering imp.

Somehow the idea of Rebel being polite bothered Athena almost as much as him being his usual vicious self. It was somehow unnatural, and she was certain it meant trouble. For instance, it was difficult to guess what he had learned from tormenting her and her family through the Internet. Had they unwittingly participated in some pilot project? Who would he torment now? She hoped his next target would not be her problem.

While she pondered, the phone rang. In a moment her mother came to her door. "Jason," she said.

"Jason?" Athena said when she picked up the receiver. "Great news. Rebel gave us back control of our lives."

"Cool," Jason said. "But we have bigger problems now." He sounded tense and worried.

"Like what?" Athena asked. She'd caught his mood right through the telephone.

"You know that Sixth Column stuff?"

"Yes?"

"It's big, Ath," he said. "It's big and it's bad." He paused, then said, "And it's going down tonight."

chapter eleven@cybersurfers.ghost

chapter eleven@cybersurfers.ghost

Jason sat before his computer at home scrolling eye-over-eye through the muddy prose of the files he had pulled off the secret Sixth Column conference. It was complicated military stuff containing documents unlike those in any game he'd ever seen. He didn't understand most of what the maps and documents said, but he got the impression the people who did the writing took it very seriously.

It looked like Sixth Column was going to attack some place in Mill Valley that very night. He had no idea where or why, but Rebel's practical jokes seemed like small potatoes compared to what these geeks had in mind.

He became excited when he found a section he could actually understand. If he was reading the section correctly, these Sixth Column guys were even loonier than he had suspected. He printed it out and read it again.

23. During Phase One, our codes and passwords will demonstrate their usefulness breaking through the Internet firewalls of a small local bank, of a regional phone company, of the country's largest clearing house of credit information, and of the military forces who do the bidding of those currently in power.

24. Using the information gathered during Phase One we will proceed to Phase Two: the disruption of life throughout the country, demonstrating the basic corruption of the system.

25. During Phase Three we will heroically take power, saving the country from chaos.

Jason had trouble taking this stuff seriously. It sounded as if Sixth Column wanted to mess things up, blame the confusion on the government, then step in and save everybody. It was like the plot of a bad science fiction movie, *Plan Nine from the Internet*.

Phase One sounded an awful lot like what Rebel had done to Athena and her family. The whole anti-Bergstrom rumpus was obviously a test case to see if Sixth Column's "bugs" worked—and they did. It also seemed pretty clear now that Susan was Rebel, and that Rebel's nonsense was a sort of trial run for Sixth Column's big plans. Susan didn't like Athena and that was why she picked her for the target, even bringing Jason into it. No wonder Susan was visiting Bruce, he realized as he leaned back in his chair. The two conspirators certainly had a lot to discuss.

If Sixth Column was into Phase One already,

could Phase Two be far behind? The thought of these guys taking over the country frightened Jason. He was sure—or hoped—they wouldn't stand a chance, but they could sure do a lot of damage trying. He and Athena had to stop them. But how?

Athena had already convinced Jason that going after Bruce at this time was pointless. His cover story, and the fact that he was nearly an adult, gave him an edge. On the other hand, Susan seemed like a good prospect. Jason thought he could frighten her by showing her that he knew some of Sixth Column's secrets.

She would panic and run to Bruce to warn him that they had been exposed. He and Athena and the police would be in the next room listening, and ba-ba-ba-bing! End of revolution.

They would all get medals, maybe meet the President, and then go home for a nice dinner. Excited by his own vision, Jason called Susan and invited her over for a little Sixth Columning.

"I'll be right over," she said, sounding pleased and not a little triumphant.

Jason hung up. Let her have her triumph, he thought as he rubbed his hands together mad-doctor style. It would be totally temporary.

He figured he had about twenty minutes before Susan arrived. During that time he studied the Sixth Column maps and text files, but could still make no more out of them. He got a glass of water and set it near the computer. Susan would need it, or so he hoped.

The doorbell rang. When Jason opened it, Susan leaped into his arms and gave him a long slow kiss right on the button. He let it go on for a while, and then with some difficulty finally pushed her away.

"Er, hi, Susan. Nice to see you, too. I have Sixth Column all ready." He untangled himself from her embrace and started up the stairs without looking back. He had no idea what Susan was thinking, but a moment later he heard her start up after him.

He sat down in one of the two chairs in front of his computer. She sat down next to him and gazed at him appraisingly, eyebrows up, tiny tight-mouthed smile. "You really want to play Sixth Column?" she asked.

"For a while," Jason said. "We'll see what happens. It's a long evening." He flashed her what he hoped was a winning grin.

She nodded.

"I have a password," Jason said, "that'll get us into places we can't usually go." Feeling confident, he brought up the Sixth Column game, and logged on. The normal game screen appeared, but when he typed in SNAFU, they dropped into the secret level.

Jason leaned back and let Susan do the maneuvering. She seemed engrossed. When she came to the map of Mill Valley she stopped.

"How did this stuff get here?" Susan demanded. Jason had expected a fearful tone of voice. Her expression of outraged decency threw him off a little.

"The same way *this* stuff got here," he said, and clicked onto one of the text screens.

She read a few words, then grabbed Jason by

the wrist. It was not a sign of affection. "How did this stuff get here?" she asked again.

"I guess you know what it is," Jason said, still trying to act casual, though his plan was not going the way he expected it to.

"Of course," Susan said, "it's . . . " She stopped, blinked, and read a little more. She took the mouse from Jason and began surfing through the maps and text documents. She was a woman on a mission. Jason didn't know what was going on.

"Well, I'm confused," she said at last, frowning at the monitor.

"Why?" Jason asked, a little confused himself.

"Tell me how this stuff got here." She was glaring at him now, no longer the fun-loving Susan he'd known. If they were going to move this conversation off the dime, one of them would have to give.

"I don't know," Jason said. "I suppose Bruce put it there."

"Damn!" Susan shouted at the ceiling. "He told me he wanted that stuff for the game!"

"He did?" Jason asked. "Bruce lied to you?"

"I'd say so. He told me he wanted some accurate military information to spice up his game, and like a dolt I got it from my dad's files and gave it to him. And from the look of things," she tapped the screen, "he's going to use that military information tonight!"

Jason stared at her. Whatever was going on, Athena had earned the right to be part of it. "Hold that thought," he said, and picked up his bedside phone to call Athena. He explained the situation and she promised to be right over.

"You and Athena are really tight," Susan stated.

"Pretty tight," Jason admitted. "All the Rebel stuff just pushed us closer together."

"Who's Rebel?" Susan asked.

"I thought you were," Jason replied.

"Well, I'm not," she came back at him angrily. "Were you just using me?"

"Susan, there's no time to argue right now," Jason said. "We can talk about that later."

"Fine. Who's Rebel?" she repeated.

The bottom dropped out of Jason's stomach. Susan waited patiently while he took a couple of sips of the water he'd put out for her. She wasn't faking, he was sure of that. She really had no idea who Rebel was. She might be in a lot of trouble, too.

"Look," Jason said, "I'd like to have this conversation right now, but Athena will be here in a few minutes, and I'd like her to get involved in this. OK?"

"I don't want to play Sixth Column while we wait," Susan said.

"Me neither. How 'bout some hot chocolate?"

They went downstairs to the kitchen and Jason started to boil water. When it was hot a few minutes later Jason mixed it with chocolate powder in a couple of mugs. He and Susan did not talk much. They didn't even look at each other much. Jason was thinking about Rebel and Sixth Column and what it might be like to date Susan now that he'd found out she was a real person. He and Athena weren't dating, after all. They were just friends—cyberbuds.

The doorbell rang for the second time that

evening. "What's the rumpus?" Athena asked as Jason opened the door.

"It's kind of complicated," he said, leading her into the kitchen.

Athena stopped dead when she saw Susan.

Susan regarded her calmly, sipping her drink.

"I don't know what the two of you have cooked up," Athena said angrily, "but I don't want to have any part of it." She turned to go.

"It's not what you think. Not this time, anyway," Susan said. She was obviously not going to let Jason off the hook that easily.

"Oh," Athena said. "So now you're some kind of mind reader." She was stiff with rage, her fists balled at her sides.

"We were talking about Rebel," Jason said.

"Yes," Susan said. "Jason thinks I'm Rebel."

Athena turned around and took a step into the kitchen, obviously interested despite herself. Jason was relieved to see that Susan's unaggressive tone had soothed her.

"She's not Rebel," Athena said. "I think it's Bruce."

"Bruce?" Jason thought for a few moments. His face suddenly brightened. "Bruce! Now that makes sense," Jason agreed.

"What makes you think so?" Susan asked.

"What are you doing here, Susan?" Athena interrupted, changing the subject.

"Jason thought I was Rebel—whoever that is. Or he thought I was involved with some dirty games Sixth Column is playing. Or something."

"She's been really helpful," Jason explained, trying to ease up the tension in the room without alienating either woman. He turned to Susan. "How do you know so much?" he asked.

Susan looked him in the eye. "My dad is Colonel Hunter. He's the commanding officer overseeing the Army maneuvers in Mill Valley."

"An army brat!" Athena exclaimed.

"You betcha," Susan said.

"Give me some water," Athena said as she took off her coat and hung it over the back of a chair. Jason hopped to it.

"Bruce has to be Rebel because he's the only one around who both knows me," Athena said while Jason handed her a glass of water, "and has access to the USX codes and passwords."

Jason nodded. Susan still looked a little bewildered. Athena explained what Rebel had been doing to her for the past week or so.

"Poor kid," Susan said and laid her hand on Athena's. Athena didn't look comfortable with the contact, but she didn't move away either.

Jason was relieved things were so cozy until a sudden thought made him stand up nervously. "I'm glad we're all one big happy family. But I think that Sixth Column is going to do their thing tonight."

Susan's eyes widened in shock and she ran from the room. Jason and Athena leapt up the stairs right behind her. When they entered Jason's bedroom, Susan was at his computer searching through text files.

"Here it is," she said. "Twenty-one thirty hours."

"What is supposed to happens at 21:30 hours?" Athena asked.

"Well, according to this," Susan said as she perused the text, "Sixth Column is going to try interrupting Satcom and feed bad coordinates to the Army's mobile computers."

"What's Satcom?" Athena asked.

"Satcom is a network of orbiting space satellites that covers the globe," Jason explained. "They can tell you exactly where you are—and where your target is."

"Meaning what?" Athena asked.

"Meaning Sixth Column wants to discredit the government by misleading the Army into blowing up a real farmhouse instead of the established target."

"Phase Two," Jason explained.

"That's terrible," Athena said. "Somebody could get killed."

"Bring up that map of Mill Valley again, Susan," Jason said. "Let's take a look at the target they're giving the Army."

Susan did a little fancy clicking with the mouse and in short order she had the map of Mill Valley up on the screen. "The coordinates are here," she said and moved the mouse's pointer to a spot near the intersection of two county roads.

"Oh no," Athena exclaimed, "that has to be the Henderson place!"

"Figures," Jason said. "They want to cause damage, but they don't want any real casualties." He looked at Susan and explained, "The Hendersons are away on vacation. Their farm is deserted."

"Wrong," Athena said grimly. The panic inside her was echoed in her voice. "Tracy is out there!

She's house-sitting right in the middle of ground zero!"

chapter twelve@cybersurfers.cybercops
chapter twelve@cybersurfers.cybercops
chapter twelve@cybersurfers.cybercops

"We need a fast car!" Athena cried as she threw the phone onto Jason's bed.

"Even if we had one, we can't drive. And we wouldn't make it in time," Susan said as she checked her watch. "Twenty-one thirty hours is nine-thirty. We have less than half an hour."

"Why don't we just call her and tell her to get out of there?" Jason asked.

"We can't," Athena exclaimed, on the verge of tears. "Her phone's been disconnected!"

Jason nodded. "Then we'll have to do what we should have done in the first place. We'll have to hack. Let me at that keyboard."

"Wait a minute," Susan said. "I'd like to try something else first."

"Hurry!" Athena cried when Susan picked up the phone from the bed and started to dial.

"Hi, Mom?" Susan said into the phone. "Dad's long gone, isn't he? That's what I thought. Is there any way to contact him in the field? None? Are you sure? OK, Mom. Thanks. I'll tell you later. See you soon." Susan sat on the bed, wilted. "Sometimes I hate Army protocol."

"Can we hack now?" Jason cried.

"Be my guest," Susan said. "But you'll need these." She quickly scribbled some passwords that Jason would need to get through the Army's firewalls.

"Glad you're on our side," he said as he read the passwords. Athena watched as he entered the first one into the computer, his fingers flying across the keyboard at lightning speed.

```
***** CONNECT *****

The password works. You're inside the military
planning system . . . or at least the local com-
mand center.
    Now let's see what the Army is planning to
target for their field test. . . .
    There are the coordinates, they're almost
exactly where Satcom has the Henderson farm
located. But why?
    No way to tap into the Satcom system itself and
change numbers . . . so Bruce is doing something
else. What?
    That's it. Right in front of you . . . and so
simple.

***** INTERRUPT *****
```

"What's happening?" Athena asked, filled with anxiety. She hated being in the dark when crazy stuff was going on.

"Bruce has added one little glitch to the program, which changes everything," Jason said. "The real coordinates are being fed in from Satcom, but he's added a little routine that changes the numbers so that they locate a different target."

"Like the Henderson farm," Susan said.

"Right. His program has a self-destruct command so it won't be there when they start investigating what went wrong. Everything will check out fine—except the Army blew up the wrong house."

"Tracy's in that house," Athena repeated. She couldn't bear the thought of Tracy being the innocent victim of some sick cyberspace militiaperson's maneuvers. "You have to stop them!"

***** RECONNECT *****

Stopping them is easy now that you know where the bomb is hidden.

Defuse it . . . but carefully, so you don't disrupt the rest of the system. Done.

Bypass the number-changing routine so what Satcom sends in, the Army reads out.

Now erase Bruce's little program . . .

Wait! Better idea.

Disarm it but leave it so it can be found . . . one

```
more cybernail in Bruce's coffin.
Done.


***** DISCONNECT *****
```

"That does it," Jason said, as he sat back in his chair, everything on his body slumping. Athena knew from watching him in past crises that hacking was hard work when you were racing against a deadline.

Athena was exhausted, too. Even Susan looked drained—an interesting change from her usual sexy chipperness, Athena noted. Made her almost seem like a normal person.

They'd done everything they could, but Athena was still nervous, knowing that Tracy's life was at stake. "It's 9:15," she said, looking at her watch. "I think you can call the police now, Jason."

"Right," Jason said and started typing again.

"I got so involved with the computer stuff," Susan said, "I didn't even think of the police. Why didn't we call them before?"

"I wanted them to catch Bruce in the act of messing with the Army's information and security systems. I didn't want there to be any question about what he was doing."

"Sure. He could claim he was just playing a game," Athena said.

"Right."

Both women watched Jason.

"How does he know how to get into the police network?" Susan asked.

"I'm a genius," Jason said without stopping what he was doing.

Athena smiled and shook her head. "When the police asked Jason to set up the Cyberhut they gave him a couple of access codes into their system. Using those, he found out others. Bruce must have hacked into the police system using Jason's computer at school." Athena shrugged. "But Jason still might be a genius," she added warmly.

"What's the Cyberhut?" asked Susan.

"It's a place on the Internet where kids can hang out online," Athena answered. "Jason's building it."

Susan nodded.

A few minutes later Jason turned around in his chair. "That was easy," he said. "It turns out the police knew that the FBI has had their eyes on Sixth Column for a long time. The cybercops are on their way to Lock-Me-Tight Systems." He grinned. "It's going to be quite a party."

"Will they catch Bruce in the act?" Athena asked.

"Trust me. There's no way he can cover all his tracks," Jason said. He stared at Athena. "Why are you biting your lip, Ath? We took care of everything."

"I know," Athena said. "But I'd feel better if I could talk to Tracy."

"The police are on their way out there right now," Jason said.

The next morning Athena lay in bed trying to decide if she felt any different having helped save the United States from a gang of home-grown wackos. She felt good about it, of course, but she still felt like a high-school kid, not like James Bond. Of course, she had no idea how James Bond felt when he awoke in the morning. Besides, she still didn't know what had actually happened, whether the police had made it to Lock-Me-Tight Systems in time to catch Bruce in the act of being himself.

Then she remembered Tracy. She hadn't been able to get her friend on the phone the night before, and it had been too late to go out there, but Jason had assured her Tracy would be fine.

Tracy would still be housesitting at the Henderson's for another two days, so they wouldn't be walking to school together. Athena decided to make a point of running into her during the day.

During the week, breakfast was a free-for-all meal—everybody made their own. Dad and Ralph were sitting at the table eating corn flakes and discussing football, and Mom was musing over something while standing at the sink drinking coffee.

"Hey, guys," Athena said as she walked into the kitchen.

Grunts all around.

Would they believe her if she told them about the adventure of the previous night? Maybe if she posted a note on the family bulletin board. She could just see it in her mind: Hi, guys. The reason your daughter was a little late getting home last night is that she was making the world safe for democracy.

Her family members might be polite about it, but they would never believe her, not even if she said, "No, really!" a lot. Just one more Internet fantasy.

The *Fort Benson Commercial* was on the table, ignored in favor of the *New York Times*, which her dad preferred.

When Athena saw the headline on the front page of the *Commercial* she picked it up eagerly and read the story. It was even more exciting because it was written by Art Menkin, a reporter Athena and Jason had actually met in one of their previous adventures involving cyberspace.

COPS NAB TERRORISTS
by Art Menkin

(*Special to the* Commercial)—Last night a combined action of the Fort Benson police and the FBI stopped a plot that could have had wide-ranging and dangerous consequences for the entire nation.

Tipped off by an anonymous informant, the Fort Benson police learned of a plot by Sixth Column, a paramilitary organization, to embarrass the United States Army. This was believed to be an early step leading to Sixth Column's larger objective of taking over the entire United States government.

The police first thought the report was a prank, but the fact that the informant was known to them, and that the FBI had been watching Sixth Column for some time confirmed that the report was real.

Under the command of Federal Agent Phil Marlowe, FBI agents, and Fort Benson police surrounded building twenty-seven of Benson Heights Industrial Park and tapped into the phone line of Lock-Me-Tight Systems, a well-known computer and mainframe security firm. As their informant had reported, information in military code was flowing between a computer inside the Lock-Me-Tight offices and the computers controlling the military maneuvers near Mill Valley.

Allegedly, the intention of Sixth Column was to cause the army to shell a private farmhouse instead of the actual target, a shack on military property. The owners of the farmhouse were away on vacation, but it was inhabited by a young high-school student who had been hired to house-sit.

Federal Agent Marlowe and his team raided the Lock-Me-Tight offices and found a young man named Bruce Archer watching the data flow between the military computers and the computer before which he sat. Archer did not put up a fight, and he seemed surprised that anyone would bother with what he allegedly considered to be no more than a practical joke. With the shutting down of Archer's operation, the Army once again turned its attention to the correct target. Neither the high-school student nor the farmhouse was harmed.

When taken into custody, Archer said, "I was working for these Sixth Column bozos because it was fun. I didn't think that they actually had any chance of taking over the country."

This reporter observed Agent Marlowe shaking his head. "Even if Archer is telling the truth, he is still guilty of being an irresponsible citizen who did not consider the dire consequences of his actions."

According to authorities, Archer has promised to help in any way he can with an investigation of Sixth Column.

Ms. O'Malley sure won't like any of that, Athena thought, feeling a delicious thrill.

"Did you guys see this?" Athena asked, holding up the paper.

Ralph squinted at the print. "Yeah. Crazy, huh? I thought stuff like that just happened in the big bad city."

"It's a goofy world," Mr. Bergstrom remarked and took another spoonful of cereal.

Athena couldn't argue with that.

As she walked into the school building, she almost ran into Ms. O'Malley hurrying out.

"Excuse me, Athena," Ms. O'Malley said. "I'm in something of a hurry."

"Sorry to hear about your nephew, Bruce," was all Athena could think of to say.

"You saw that libel in the paper, did you? I'm sure it's some kind of mistake. I'm going to the police station right now to see what I can do to clear up this error," Ms. O'Malley stated officiously.

Good luck, Athena thought. "Ms. O'Malley,"

she called after her cautiously, "what did you finally decide about the Internet gateway here at school?"

"Mr. Madison convinced me to leave it open. He can be quite a spellbinder. And now, if you'll excuse me . . ." She dashed down the steps.

Well, well, Athena thought. More good news.

As it turned out, she and Tracy didn't cross paths until lunch. When Athena saw her alive, well, and perky as usual, she couldn't help herself—she ran to Tracy and engulfed her in a big hug.

"What's the matter, Ath?" Tracy asked, overwhelmed. "You look as if you're about to cry."

"Nothing anymore," Athena said as she tried to control her trembling. "Did you have a nice evening last night?"

"Great. I actually got some studying done. The phone company was doing repairs, so no one called. The only weird thing was when the police stopped by and asked me if I was all right. They even stayed for a bit to keep me company. It was heaven—at least for one night," she said. "Why do you ask?"

"Oh, you know, the Army exercises and all. I thought they might have kept you awake."

"Didn't hear a thing. But those cute Army guys never did come back," Tracy sighed.

For once Tracy's boy-craziness didn't bug Athena. Athena felt light, almost fluffy. It wasn't until she entered the computer lab at the end of the day that her mood crashed. When she walked in the door Jason and Susan were sitting on desks in the center of the room, talking with their heads close together. Athena tried to put the best face she could on this situation. After all, last night the three of them had supposedly become friends.

"Hi, guys," Athena said with all the gaiety she could muster.

"Hey, Ath," Jason said. "You'll want to hear this. Susan was just explaining how she got involved with Bruce."

"I was a first-class idiot," Susan admitted, shaking her head. "I met him through Ms. O'Malley—"

"There seems to be a lot of that going around," Athena said.

"Yeah. Anyway, when he found out I was well-connected with the military he got real interested in me. That's the first time a guy asked me out because my dad was a colonel instead of despite the fact." She made a funny face and laughed.

Susan was making fun of herself, which was charming and almost endearing. Athena was finding it more and more difficult not to like her.

"When I found out Bruce was an expert on Sixth Column—the game, not the subversive activity—I was hooked, too. It turned out that while he was giving me tips on how to play the game, he was pumping me for information about the Army's maneuvers near Mill Valley, including the passwords into the system. I was an idiot—totally," Susan admitted.

"You couldn't have known," Athena offered generously.

"No. But I should have guessed," Susan

replied. "Guys like Jason don't grow on trees."

Jason smiled shyly.

"He's a hacker, all right," Athena said just to show she was still in the running.

"Uh, look," Jason said, "Mr. Madison asked me to start a project warning kids about how to avoid the bear pits on the Internet. You guys want to help?"

"Sure," Athena and Susan said together.

The two girls looked at each other through narrowed eyes. Athena knew what Susan was thinking because she was thinking the same thing. Guys like Jason sure didn't grow on trees. And neither do girls like me, Athena thought, sitting down at the terminal next to Jason's while Susan flanked him on the other side. Neither do girls like me.

Internet.notes

Finding your way around the Internet can be confusing if you're a newbie, so here are some of Jason and Athena's "words to the wise" when you're traveling through cyberspace. This glossary has explanations, definitions, cool signs for communicating in shorthand, and some great hints about what you can expect to find online.

Q: What's a network?

A network is a group of computers joined by data-carrying links such as phone lines. A network may be as small as two or three personal computers tied together by local telephone lines in the same building, or it may be a vast complex of computers spread across the world, whose data links include telephone lines, satellite relays, fiber-optic cables, or radio links.

Q: What's the Internet?

In the beginning there was the ARPANET, a wide-area experimental network that linked universities and government research labs together. Over time other groups formed their own networks. The collection of all of these different networks joined together became what we call the Internet.

Q: What's FTP mean and what is it?

File Transfer Protocol (FTP for short) allows you to get files from other computers, or to send files to another computer.

Q: What's a Telnet?

The network terminal protocol (Telnet) allows you to log on to any other computer on the network. From the time you log on until you finish the session, every character you type is sent directly to the other system just as if you were actually sitting there.

Q: What's e-mail and how much postage does it need?

E-mail is electronic mail that you send to friends on other computers. It can be in the form of typed messages or graphic images. You don't even need a postage stamp, just your computer and your keyboard. And it gets there a lot faster than "snail mail," which is how computer users refer to regular post office service.

Q: What's the Usenet?

Usenet is a collection of newsgroups that are devoted to the particular interests of a group of people. Newsgroups might discuss the environment or the latest science-fiction gossip. There's a Usenet newsgroup for almost everything.

Q: What's the World Wide Web?

The Web is not the only service on the Internet, but it's rapidly becoming one of the most popular. It's got pictures and hypertext— which means you can jump from one place to another, all over the world, with a single click of your computer's mouse.

Q: What's a Freenet?

These are bulletin board systems that are connected to the Internet and are free of charge. Usually a Freenet is sponsored by community groups to give people free access to computing and information.

Q: What's CERT?

The Computer Emergency Response Team is a security force for the Internet that maintains a clearinghouse for information about network security, including attempted—or successful—break-ins to private (or commercial) networks or bulletin board systems.

Q: What's meant by netiquette?

This is simply the proper way to behave when you're surfing the Internet, such as respecting the rights and opinions of others, and treating others the way you want to be treated.

Q: What's freeware?

This is software that you may use and give to your friends without paying for it—and it's legal to do so.

Q: What's shareware?

This is like freeware and it doesn't cost you anything to get and try out. But if you like it and want to use it, then you send the author of the program a small licensing fee.

Q? What's an FAQ?

That's a Frequently Asked Question, and it usually refers to a file that contains FAQs about a particular subject in a particular system.

Q: What's a MUD?

MUDs (Multiple User Dimensions) are role-playing games. MUDs exist on the Internet for entertainment purposes and are essentially text-based virtual worlds that players (participants) may explore, change, or add onto. In most cases, the MUD is actually a "game" with scores, player attributes, levels, etc., but some MUDs have more social goals in mind. MUDs are usually based on different science fiction genres such as fantasy, space, or even cyberpunk.

Q: What's an IRC?

An IRC, or Internet Relay Chat, allows you to "chat" online—in real time using typing rather than speaking—with other computer users all over the world.

Q: What's a smiley?

When you're face-to-face, you can smile, frown, or make any number of facial expressions to enhance your words. You can also sound happy, sad, angry, or just plain bored by it all. In e-mail your words have to carry your thoughts by themselves—so folks invented "smileys" to punctuate their phrases.

There are two types of basic smileys: those with words and those with pictures.

Some of the word smileys, which are always bracketed between < > include:

<grin> or just plain <g>
<frown>
<chuckle>
<smile>
<smirk> or a <wink>
even a <silly grin>

The picture smileys—look at them sideways to get the idea—include:

:-)	smile with a nose
:)	smile without a nose
;-)	wink
`-)	another wink
:*)	just clowning around
:-D	said with a smile
:-!	you put your foot in your mouth
:-,	said with a smirk
:/)	it's not funny
:-"	pursing your lips
:-r	sticking your tongue out
:-b	another sticking your tongue out
(:-&	you're angry

:,-(	crying
(:-(	sad
:-o	you're shouting, or I'm shocked
:-@	you're SCREAMING
:-(	you're unhappy
:-c	you're really unhappy
II*(	offer a handshake
II*)	accept a handshake
[?	give a hug
:-x	give a kiss

Q: What's an Acronym?

These are just shortcuts, like saying "OK" instead of "Okay," that are used in e-mail:

B4N	Bye for now
BBS	Bulletin Board System
CU	See you
CUL	See you later
DTRT	Do The Right Thing
FYI	For Your Information
FWIW	For What It's Worth
GIGO	Garbage In, Garbage Out
IMO	In My Opinion
IMHO	In My Humble Opinion
PMFJI	Pardon Me For Jumping In
SYSOP	SYStem OPerator
TIA	Thanks In Advance

Glossary

What are they talking about when they talk about:

Address. An Internet address is much like a home address, except that it is in cyberspace. An address is broken down into a few parts. For example, Athena's Internet address is: athena@gateway.net. Her user name is *athena*. She lives in the Internet at (@) the domain (think of domain as a cybertown) called *gateway. net* at the end of the address stands for the type of domain; there are six domain types in the United States: *com* (commercial), *edu* (educational), *mil* (military), *gov* (government), *org* (organizational), and *net* (network).

Articles. Letters that are posted in newsgroups are often referred to as articles rather than letters. This is because in mailing lists you are usually answering one person—even though everyone on the mailing list can read your letter. But in newsgroups you are often writing comments to the whole group, much like a reporter for everyone who subscribes to a magazine.

Artificial Reality. This is similar to virtual reality, but more interactive, with the participant being part of, not just passively experiencing, the artificial environment.

ASCII. Pronounced "ass-key," this stands for American Standard Code for Information Interchange. It is a universal format that allows different types of computers to understand the same information. Word processing programs often save a document in ASCII format so that another word processor on another computer will be able to understand it.

BASIC. Beginner's All-purpose Symbolic Instruction Code is relatively simple programming language often used in programming personal computers.

Baud. Bit per second. Used to measure the speed of data transfer.

BBS. Bulletin Board Systems are networks that your computer can dial into through your modem. You communicate with other people

Cybercops & Flame Wars

by exchanging messages and files or by transferring pictures or other information the bulletin board operator has put up for public consumption to your own computer. Transferring to your computer is called *downloading*.

Beta test. This refers to testing computer software after it has been developed but before it is sold to the general public. The first testing stage, *alpha*, is usually done by the company that develops the program. The second testing stage, *beta*, is handled by a carefully chosen group of people outside the company. When you beta test a product, you can give the company your opinion about what you like and don't like about their program. Beta tests are given to see if a program really works in your home the way it did in the lab.

Bootleg. An unauthorized copy of computer software. This is illegal.

Boot up. You do this when you start up your computer by turning on the power.

Continuous loop. This is a section of a computer that is repeated over and over again and can't be interrupted.

CPU. A Central Processing Unit is the brains of a computer. Also called *microprocessor* or just *processor*.

Cursor. Usually a blinking box or line on your computer screen. It indicates where the next character will be inserted.

Cybercops. This can be any agency that pretects data online. Most often it refers to the U. S. Secret Service.

Cyberian. This is an online librarian who makes a living doing information research and retrieval. Cyberians are cyberspace's really hot data surfers.

Cyberpunk. A subcategory of science fiction launched in 1982 by William Gibson's novel, *Neuromancer*.

Cyberspace. This is where you go when you go online. It's the universe that exists inside computer networks. You can't see it, but it's there—and you can visit it.

Data. Information that has been formatted so that it can be understood by a computer. This can include text, numbers, program code, graphic art, and sound.

Debugging. To correct errors in software.

Delurking. This is when you stop lurking online; you join the conversation. (See **Lurking**.)

Digital. Computers "talk" to other computers digitally. That is, they store and process information as a series of numbers. Anything—including words, pictures, and sounds—can be "digitized" with a software program—like a word processor—so you can read the words, hear the sounds, or see the pictures.

Directory. If you think of the hard disk on your computer as a filing cabinet, then the directories are like drawers in that cabinet.

Domain. (See **Address**.)

Download. This is when you transfer data from a larger computer system to a smaller system. Usually done through a modem.

E-mail. (See page 130.)

Encode. Coding a computer file or disk with a password.

Encrypted file. These files are copy protected so that they either can't be opened or read.

Feeb. A real incompetent at something, as in "I'm a real feeb when it comes to math."

Firewall. A protective barrier to prevent unauthorized intruders from penetrating your computer system.

Flame. To flame someone is to stomp on someone in cyberspace for saying something you consider wrong or just plain stupid. It's kind of like slamming the door when you're mad.

Gateway. This is a connection that allows one network to pass information to another network or to a mainframe computer.

Glitch. Means a small problem in the computer program, which often results in big problems in the output.

Gofer. Slang for someone who Goes For things.

Cybercops & Flame Wars

Grrrl. Slang for a female cyberpunk.

Hacker. This is slang for someone who may have a degree in computer science, but who has gained most of his or her computer expertise through trial and error, learning to navigate in cyberspace in places not usually taught about in computer classes.

Handle. The code name a person might use on the Net.

Hardware. Any part of your computer that you can touch is hardware, such as the screen, hard disk, keyboard, etc. (The rest is software.)

Hyperlink. This is the link used in hypertext documents to jump from one element to another.

Hypertext. These are links in documents that point to other documents. When you're reading a hypertext document (on the World Wide Web, for example) you can quickly jump to a linked document for related information—then jump back.

Icarus. This is a made-up name for an Internet gateway program that Jason and Athena learn to use in Cybersurfers #1: *Pirates on the Internet.*

Icon. A small image or picture on a screen that selects and executes a program (or a function within a program) when you click on it with a mouse.

Ident. Cybertalk shorthand for identity.

Identity hacking. The use of pseudo-anonymity or false accounts to pass one's self off as another person on the Internet. Not nice.

Imp. In cybertalk, an imp is a mischievous little program that performs a certain set of functions.

Initialize. To start up a program or system.

Interactive. This describes the two-way dialogue between computer programs and you. In other words, when you do something the computer responds and then returns control back to you. Interactive computer games are games in which you can affect the outcome.

LAN. Local Area Networks are used to connect several computers in the same location—like in a school—together.

Listserver. Someone who is in charge of a particular informational mailing list and distributes the list to others. The name comes from the program they use for this task, called *listserver*.

Log on. This is what you do when you use your computer to connect to a network or online service. The network asks for your password, then after you type it in, tells you you're logged on.

Lurking. Hanging around in the background and watching online discussions without getting involved. Most of us are lurkers when we first enter a new neighborhood on the Internet.

Microchip. Usually made of silicon, a microchip can be the size of your fingernail and can store huge amounts of information or program instructions for the computer.

Modem. This is a simple way of saying modulator-demodulator. It is a device used to connect a computer through a phone line to other computers that may be thousands of miles away.

MOO. An Object-Oriented MUD, that includes pictures as well as words.

Motherboard. This is the common name used for the main circuit board inside a computer. It contains the CPU, memory, and port connections to printers, disk drives, etc.

Mouse. A device used to move the cursor around the screen. Most mouse devices have two buttons that you click to make selections and issue commands.

MUDs. Multiple User Dimensions are online environments, usually games, where several players can participate at once.

Net. This is simply shorthand for the Internet.

Nethead. Someone who spends a lot of time on the Internet and knows a lot about it.

Netsurfer. Someone who browses the Net. (See **Surfer.**)

Newbie. A new kid on the block. We are all newbies when we're first learning our way around the Internet.

Cybercops & Flame Wars

Newsgroups. Newsgroups are online gatherings in which you can discuss almost any subject you can imagine—from how to house-train your pet to what the latest UFO rumor is. There are currently over 10,000 active newsgroups.

Ohnosecond. That terrible moment in time when you realize you've just made a BIG mistake—like erasing all the files in the wrong subdirectory.

Online. Describes computers that are directly connected to a CPU and ready to communicate through phone lines. Also, when you are online, you are in cyberspace.

Pipeline. In computer terms it means the connection the data flows through.

Processor chip. This is a microchip that processes instructions for the computer. (See **CPU**.)

RAM. Random Access Memory is the computer's "working" memory; it works all the time when your computer is on. It can be accessed quickly and is used to store programs that are currently running.

Read / write head. This is a device that retrieves data from or writes data on a hard or floppy disk.

Real space. This is simply the opposite of cyberspace and refers to our real world where you physically live.

Real time. Real time is the actual moment you are living in now. Think of it like being on the phone as opposed to writing a letter. When you are on the phone, you can ask a question and get an answer immediately in real time. Conversely, when you write a letter, you have to wait for the postal carrier to pick it up, the post office to route and deliver it, and the recipient to read it—all before you can get an answer.

Reboot. To re-start a computer.

ROM. Read-Only Memory. ROM contains programs that are necessary for your computer to work. This memory stays even when you turn off the computer.

Satcom. A network of orbiting space satellites around the globe that can tell you exactly where you are—anywhere on the planet.

SNAFU. Stands for Situation Normal, All Fouled Up!

Squawk box. A small loudspeaker used for public address systems.

Subdirectory. If a directory is like a drawer in a filing cabinet, then subdirectories are like folders containing information such as programs or documents inside the drawers. (See **Directory**.)

Surfer. This term is borrowed from athletes who ride the ocean's waves on surfboards. In cyberspace, a surfer is someone who glides from site to site, exploring and watching, playing, and maybe even hacking.

Sysop. Means SYStem OPerator and refers to someone running a computer bulletin board or other online system. Sysops are always ready to come to your rescue if you don't understand part of their system.

Terminate-and-stay resident. Refers to programs that load into memory and stay there until needed. These are calendars or phone lists and are called up by hitting a special key combination.

TinyMUD. A socially oriented MUD where people do more talking rather than battling dragons.

Upload. When you transfer data from your computer to a remote (usually larger) computer system. (See **Download**.)

Virtual Reality. (Also known as VR.) This is a world that exists only in cyberspace. Modern day virtual reality uses helmets, gloves, and body suits to create an environment that is connected to the virtual reality devices through a computer. A goal of some virtual reality researchers is to generate a completely alternate reality. The possibilities of VR-generated environments are as limitless as the imagination.

Web. This is simply shorthand for the World Wide Web.

Web browser. These are programs that let you navigate through the World Wide Web and see graphics and text on your computer screen. They also allow you to make hypertext leaps to other Web sites. There are many other Web-browser software programs, and when you sign up to get onto the Net, the company you sign up with usually sends you a Web-browser software program to get started.

Windows™ 95. Microsoft's popular graphical interface operating system.

Wonk. A jerk who just doesn't get the message.

ABOUT THE AUTHORS

TED PEDERSEN began his literary career writing programs for computers in Seattle before making the long trek south to Los Angeles, where he switched to writing for the even weirder world of television. His most recent credits include episodes for the animated series *X-Men*, *Spider-Man*, *Skysurfer Strike Force*, and *ExoSquad*. His second *Deep Space Nine* young adult novel, *Gypsy World*, has just been published, and he is currently writing the script for an interactive multimedia game. When not surfing the net, Ted lives in Venice, California, with his wife, Phyllis, and an accumulation of cats and computers.

MEL GILDEN has written two adult novels in the Star Trek universe, *Boogeymen* and *The Starship Trap*, plus the *Deep Space Nine* young adult book, *The Cardassian Imps*. He's the author of many books for kids, most recently the *My Brother Blubb* series, and his latest hardcover, *The Pumpkins of Time*. In his spare time, he's written animated cartoons and hosted radio shows. He lives in Los Angeles, California.

Ted and Mel previosly teamed up to write the Deep Space Nine novel, *The Pet*, as well as the first Cybersurfers novels, *Pirates on the Internet*, *Cyberspace Cowboys*, and *Ghost on the Net*.